MONEY
FAUCET

Get the Water Street Crime Starter Library
FOR FREE

Sign up for the no-spam newsletter and get *four* full-length ebooks—the thrillers **BLOODY PARADISE**, **FROM ICE TO ASHES**, **TROPICAL ICE**, and **SING FOR THE DEAD**—plus two introductory short stories by the author of **STAINED FORTUNE** and **MONEY FAUCET** and lots more exclusive content, all for *free*.

Details can be found at the end of *MONEY FAUCET*, or go here now:
mailchi.mp/waterstreetpressbooks.com/ waterstreetcrimemailinglist

MONEY FAUCET

JOE CALDERWOOD

Water Street Press
Healdsburg, California

Published by Water Street Press
Healdsburg, California

Water Street Press paperback edition published 2019

Produced in the USA

Print 978-1-62134-419-3
E-Pub 978-1-62134-420-9
Mobi 978-1-62134-421-6

Cover design by **thecovercollection.com**

Typesetting services by **bookow.com**

In loving memory of Mom, a member of the greatest generation.

Acknowledgments

I want to thank Cynthia Drew who, ten years ago, believed in my short story that became the Clint Kennedy Series.

Chapter 1

HALLOWEEN. All Hallow's fucking Eve. I stood in the office of a dead lawyer. Adrenaline, long my drug of choice, pumped through my body like a mariachi band playing in my brain. The body slumped in the cheap, cocoa-brown, vinyl-covered office chair behind the badly battered, olive-green metal desk, and the head—what was left of it; what wasn't spattered on the fake oak paneling behind the ugly desk—was thrown back against the headrest, his eyes wide open, frozen in shock at his own demise. A jointed paper skeleton hung over the window on the far side of the office and danced in the breeze from the air condition-ing unit directly beneath it—an homage to the season contributed, no doubt, by the attorney's secretary, a dowdy woman I'd found strange and irritating on the one occasion we'd met. Someone had replaced a broken pane in the window with cardboard and duct tape, probably... What was her name? Carla?

The lamp on the dead man's desk burned dimly,

throwing patches of eerie light over the blood spatters on his argyle-patterned polo shirt, the lap of his khaki pants, the unopened McDonald's paper bag that sat before him on the desk. One of his legs—the one he limped on—was propped by the heel on the top of an upturned waste can. The details hit me like a series of photographs— click, click, click—and each image burned into my brain. I would never again believe a witness to a crime who says he didn't see anything.

I panted fiercely, as if I'd just run a hard ten miles in ninety-degree heat. And the sweat—instantaneous and profuse. I could smell myself, the scent of exertion. Or was it the stink of fear? I suddenly understood why some people piss themselves when they panic, though I had not yet descended that far into distress.

"Shit, shit, shit!" I didn't know what to do. My instinct was to call the police, but the dead lawyer was an adversary of mine at the time of his demise —I had plenty of reasons to want him dead and I don't know if the cops would buy my story: *This is the way I found him when I walked in.* Which was true.

"Coulter!" I'd shouted as I'd walked in through his office door. The front office had been empty, as I'd expected it to be at that hour of the night, so I'd shouted again. "Coulter! Answer me! Where the hell are you?"

Jessie Coulter had acquiesced to my insistence that he and I, surely two reasonable men, could broker an agreement to settle our dispute without having to drag it through the court; he'd agreed to meet with me one last time. Alone. At his office. At ten o'clock at night. When everyone else in the entire shoddy strip mall where his practice was located would be gone for the day. But the timing was my fault; I'd insisted he meet me today, before I flew back home to Mérida after what had turned out to be a week's involuntary vacation in Miami, but I wouldn't cut short my Halloween celebration with the Cohens to accommodate him a few hours earlier. I was being perverse, making this shady ambulance chaser meet me on my terms. I cared deeply about the Cohen's, of course, but I didn't give a flying fuck about the holiday, and even less about seeing their grandchildren—Abe's dubious spawn—dressed up in the Harry Potter and Hermoine Granger costumes Candace had whipped up on short notice. Why did I have to be so goddamn contrary all the time? Look where it had gotten me.

I knew next to nothing about crime detection, even less about forensics, only what I'd seen on the police procedurals I sometimes caught on TV. It didn't cross my mind that no matter how suspicious the police might be of me, my innocence would, of course, be proved eventually because the lawyer would have died at an earlier hour, one for which I had an air-tight alibi—I'd been with either Jack or Xavier all day, and at the Cohens', where drink service began at five PM sharp, since the cocktail hour had started. Also, there was no murder weapon in the room to which I could be linked— Wait... I moved my eyes to scan all the surfaces in the room—the dented desk, the bare,

3

crusty floor, the rusted file cabinets, the credenza which was spattered with too much gray matter for my taste. Strangely, in the corners and along the baseboards and all among the stacks of over-stuffed file folders spread out on the floor, there was a collection of brightly colored, lint-covered jelly beans. But, no, there was no gun anywhere that I could see.

And what would I do with a gun if I found one? I had no idea. In my panic, I would probably have picked the fucking thing up and got my finger-prints all over it.

Glad there was no gun, then. Just a dead lawyer who had—gun or no gun—clearly been shot quite expertly, smack between the eyes.

Other than at funerals, at which a dead body is seen in only the most sanitized state, I'd seen only one other dead body before in my entire life. The memory of *that* murder—of finding Alvaro lifeless in my bed deep in Pablo's luxurious un-derground bunker—crept like a thick fog into my brain. I shook my head to clear it and drew in a long breath. The air in the small, closed office had the metallic tang of blood and French fry grease and I gagged. Then I slapped myself. Hard. "Pull yourself together, man. *Focus*."

At the heart of my dilemma was not a concern about eventual exoneration for the crime before me; unless someone was trying to frame me, exon-eration was a certainty. What I was worried about was the police getting all up in my business while they were figuring out I had nothing to do with the lawyer's death. That I couldn't have had anything to do with it. I had to do something—but—

What? Something more proactive than standing dumbfounded and gagging in an office with a dead bargain-basement attorney until someone —a wife? a client? that annoying secretary?— missed the slob and came looking to find out what had happened to him.

I suddenly heard a cell phone start to ring. I knew it wasn't my phone—no self-respecting criminal would be cheesy enough to use the theme from *The Sopranos* as his ring tone. But hearing the familiar tune sent another wave of adrenaline coursing through my veins. "Shit, shit, *shit!*"

Chapter 2

I am a criminal.

That's just a fact. I make my (very substantial) living performing illegal acts. Over and over again. Each weekday I transfer approximately eight million dollars of South American drug money to an American bank, thus washing, rinsing, and fluff-drying the profits of well over a dozen South American drug lords so they can legally invest their ill-gotten gains building strip malls in Tennessee and buying nursing homes in Florida. My cut is five percent. You do the math.

Did I mention I'm also a major stockholder in the American bank?

I am so filthy rich that I've been able to do something most millionaires and billionaires only dream about in their worst nightmares: philanthropy. Not the kind where you attend fancy-dress fundraising dinners or endow an already abundantly funded Ivy League university. The kind where you get your own hands dirty. My primary residence is in Mérida, Mexico's White City

—so named for its cleanliness, and the color of the paint on most of its historic buildings—and I've opened a school there that services the sons and daughters of the least among my Mexican neighbors, the Mayan kids. I've named it the Aj Tz'ib Academy—*aj tz'ib* being the Mayan word for scribe. I'd thought about naming the school for Taavi, the beautiful young Mayan who'd inspired me build it in the first place—worked his way out of his tribe's poverty all on his own, got himself a scholarship to the University of Southern Indiana and a degree in engineering, then met me and stole my whole heart in one fell swoop before falling off a bridge he was building in Kentucky and smashing his head, my heart, and all the plans he and I had made for our long and glorious future together. I would have named the school for Taavi but I didn't think I could stand seeing his name in sharp, metal letters bolted above the front entrance, or *saying* his name every time I mentioned the school, without him standing by my side. Alive.

The Aj Tz'ib Academy is a boarding school that teaches all the standard curricula to seventy-five boys and sixty-five girls between the ages of nine and sixteen, with a focus on language. As is becoming more and more the case in every country in the world, employees who can speak more than one language have an advantage over those who can speak only their native tongue. In Mexico, employees who can speak both Spanish and English are highly valued. As the Mayan kids are at the bottom rung of Mexico's ladder in any case, teaching them English gives them an enormous economic boost that might otherwise take them generations to achieve.

I am fashioning the academy from the ruins of three colonial mansions located in the center of Mérida. My own home, another lovingly restored colonial, is just blocks from the school, though I spend most of my down time in what I hope will become the hallowed halls of Aj Tz'ib. It has been nearly a year since I cut my deal with the drug lords to do their laundry, and a full eight months since I'd brought on a fellow named Tim Gustav as my assistant. Tim coordinates the armored trucks that run on a tight schedule to cartel HQs around the country, collecting drug money at each stop and transporting it back to Juan Carlos, my banker at Reforma Bank in Mérida. He also supervises each day's electronic transfers, sitting at Juan Carlos's elbow for up to six hours a day while the work is underway. Tim was a former flight attendant on a private jet—Alvaro's private jet, actually—so he has an eye for detail, as well as the innate patience, to efficiently handle these tedious tasks. In truth, if one has the necessary connections to launch such a business in the first place, and the social skills to maintain smooth relations with the drug lords themselves, there isn't a lot more to being a good launderer than that.

I had quite a bit of down time in those heady days of late 2009. And so, on the morning of October 23, 2009, I found myself in the small office at Aj Tz'ib that I shared on premises with Miguel, my contractor. I'd arrived at about ten o'clock the night before, pulled the bottle of Jameson's and the old Starbucks mug I kept in the bottom drawer of the office's desk and poured myself a healthy shot. I'd intended to put in a few hours of office work—going over the plans Miguel had drawn for the expansion of the first-floor library, approving the order of text books requested by the head master I'd hired, paying a few bills—but I'd found myself now, at 5:47 AM, still poring over the drawings, adding a balcony here, a reading nook there, and another bank of computer monitors that could fit in what I thought of as wasted space behind the librarian's station.

That was where I was when my cell phone rang —the utilitarian jangle of an old fashioned desk phone—as obsessive over my school's library as Henry the VIII had been about Nonesuch. I checked the caller ID. It was Jack, my partner in the Miami bank that accepted my dealers' Mexican funds and my best friend since we were boys growing up in Homestead, Florida. "Buddy! You're up early—"

"Clint. I'm sorry if I woke you, but— It's Dad..."

Chapter 3

THE helicopter hovered above the helipad on top of the Ryder Trauma Center in the chilly Miami dawn. Over the whoop-whoop of the rotary blades, one of the EMTs shouted, "Stable," to the surgeon who'd climbed aboard even before the landing gear made contact with the tarmac. "Not conscious," the EMT added before relaying the patient's vitals: Heart rate 90, BP 130/70, respiration 25. As the surgeon palpated the patient's abdomen, the EMT said, "Present bowel sounds, soft, non-distended."

The surgeon nodded, confirming the EMTs assessment and, taking note of what was left of the patient's silver lamé short shorts, added, "Make sure I get a tox screen with his bloodwork. Let's get him to the ER." She hoisted herself out of the aircraft. "Do we have a name?"

"Edward," a second EMT called to her. The patient had had a slim wallet tucked into the waist band of his garish shorts. The second EMT had checked it for an ID, and bagged the wallet to turn over to the police, on the short flight to Ryder

from Memorial, where an ambulance had delivered Eddie after the very first EMTs on the scene
had scraped him from the pavement.

"Stay with me, Edward," the surgeon shouted
as she ran alongside the gurney and into the hospital, holding her patient's wrist with one hand
—silently feeling for his distal pulse, buoyed by
the warmth of his extremities—shielding her eyes
from the rising, unforgiving sun with the other.
"Stay with me—"

Chapter 4

"No good deed goes unpunished."

That pithy little gem has been attributed to Noel Coward, Clare Booth Luce, Andrew Mellon and—most frequently—Oscar Wilde. Personally, I don't give a shit who said it, I don't like the sentiment. I'm the kind of guy who likes to be in control. That might seem like a funny thing to say considering my line of work, how willing I am to roll the dice, but, more often than not, I see my bets pay off. That's because I do my homework, assess a venture's downsides carefully, keep my emotions out of my business. I risk *smart*—in my commercial as well as my charitable undertakings. That's not heartless. Would you write a check to a non-profit with a questionable efficiency ratio? I write some sizeable checks to the benefit of Aj Tz'ib Academy and I like to know how my money is being spent—hence the many all-nighters I pull at the desk in the little office I share there with Miguel.

Whenever I feel too comfortably in control, however, I remember another writer, Ray Bradbury. Not only are there the vagaries of human nature to throw off the calculations of the marketplace, there's also the chaos theory to contend with. The idea that crushing one butterfly could turn the US into a fascist state has always been a little unnerving for me—far too random for my tastes. Indeed, I believe the disinclination to chaos is what gives me my inclination to preservation: the wit to make both my residence and my school from the ruins of the graceful colonial mansions that once blighted the beautiful Mérida. I like to think my efforts will help to fan the fashion away from the suburbs and toward this urban renewal, though—who knows? —perhaps I had once crushed some insect in the concrete mixed to restore a fresco or relay a native tile floor, thus throwing off the balance of the universe, and so I shoulder a measure of the burden for some tragedy that hasn't even happened yet.

But I'm getting ahead of myself. At the time the story I want to tell was taking place, we were still in the intoxicating early days of Obama's first term —there was nothing that could go wrong in the universe with such a paragon in the Oval Office, right? Don't make me laugh. Anyone who sits back on their laurels after one achievement—no matter how large or small, personal or universal —deserves everything they're going to get. If I had had advance warning about the monster fucking butterflies that were about to be unleashed in my life on the morning of October 23, 2009, I think I would have had my houseboy, Pedro, whip me up a vat of mojitos, shucked my clothes and jumped in the deep end of my pool and stayed drunk for the rest of the month.

Chalk up, among the events that should have had nothing—or at least very little—to do with me and mine, the hit-and-run that felled one Edward James "Eddie" Collier at precisely 6:43 on that morning as he tried to rollerblade across Collins Avenue at Tenth Street in South Beach. I had already received Jack's urgent telephone call by that time, and was on my way to Freeport, Bahamas, to meet him and, in any case, I hadn't seen Eddie in almost four years on the day he was run over.

Back when I was small-time, running an escort service out of Miami, Eddie had been one of my boys, and one of my favorites because my clients were crazy about him. He was cute as they come, young and always ready for adventure, but smart enough to pace himself so he always held both his end of the conversation and his liquor. I had made it a point to be friendly, but not friends, with my boys, though Eddie had made his way farther under my veneer of professional distance than any of the others because, like me, the kid was an orphan. We'd both grown up fatherless, and lost beloved mothers too early—me at twenty-two and Eddie at just fifteen. David Cohen—illustrious Miami banker, my mother's employer, and father of my best friend, Jack—had stepped in as my mentor; Eddie had been raised by his only other living relative, his grandfather, the janitor at the private school I had attended—on David's dime—with Jack. I was only a few years older than Eddie at the time he worked for me, but those few years, as well as the fact that by then I had a couple of distinguished alma maters on my resumé, gave me a leg-up in Eddie's eyes. I wasn't a father figure to him—he had his grandfather for that—or even what you'd call a mentor, mainly because I had no interest in the role, but I did act as a sort of disinterested, perpetually annoyed older brother. I took him shopping, in an effort to get him out of the outré outfits he preferred and into clothing that didn't scream rent-a-boy; the silver lamé short shorts the EMTs had had to cut off him after he was hit made me shake my head at the boy's backsliding. I put him on a budget when I discovered that, although I was paying him upwards of a grand a night, at least five nights a week, he didn't have enough credit to get himself out of one squalid room in Cutler Ridge, or buy his own car; I drove him myself to visit his grandfather in his nursing home until Eddie had saved enough to set up a life for himself. I accompanied him to see the attorney with whom I'd made an appointment to discuss his grandfather's will—not Xavier, of course; Xavier and I had already had our messy breakup by then and were still years away from an inevitable reconciliation and real friendship and, in any case, Xavier's hourly rate put him way out of Eddie's price range. No, we went to a cut-rate, family law practitioner in Hialeah because Eddie, inspired by my calls for him to take responsibility for his life and plan ahead, had been giving himself anxiety attacks with worry that his grandfather was going to outlive him and, if that happened, there would be no one to advocate for the old man's care at his cut-rate nursing home. Would I, Eddie wondered, be willing to become his grandfather's legal guardian in the case of Eddie's demise?

I was much more casual about life back in those days—mine had not yet been impacted by enough chaos, apparently, to give me a healthy respect for it. I'd shrugged and replied, "Sure. Why not?"

And therein, within that last good deed on the long list of good I'd done for my former employee, Eddie Collier, rested a good chunk of my experience of the chaos theory gone awry.

The metallic-blue, meticulously restored 1970s-era dune buggy driven by a coed with a blood alcohol level of 0.161 that ended up running over Eddie would turn out to be the vehicle that fucked up both our lives, but good.

Chapter 5

THE surgeon, Laine Gordon, tore out the clips and elastic band that had been holding her long blonde hair in a tight bun at the back of her head and ran her fingers over her scalp, massaging it vigorously, groaning with the relief of the release. Then she rolled her head in circles, three to the left and three to the right, shrugged her shoulders to loosen the tension there, bound her hair back up in the elastic band and pushed herself through the door of the CCU.

"No change, Doc," the charge nurse, Aletha, told her as she approached the nurses' station.

Laine nodded and leaned against the station, propping both arms on the high counter. "Al, what the hell happened to that kid? Fractured skull, broken arm, most of his teeth left on the street, and I still don't know that we're going to be able to save his leg…I mean, if he lives. That's the sixty-four-thousand-dollar question."

"Drunk college kid behind the wheel of a dune buggy—"

"A dune buggy did all that?"

"She was doing seventy-six miles an hour."

"On Collins Avenue?"

Aletha shrugged. "The girl was drunk, Laine."

Laine dropped her head into her hands. She'd been a practicing trauma surgeon for less than four years, and she'd seen her share of drunk-driving car accidents, but she was sure she would never be able to process the senselessness of them with any sort of professional detachment. It was almost unbearable, thinking she'd never grow any sort of self-protective carapace. "The driver walked away without a scratch, didn't she?"

Aletha sighed. "She has a bruise on her leg where her knee hit the steering column. And, of course, she was arrested."

"Oh, well, it all worked out then, didn't it?" Laine scrubbed her scalp again. "Have we been able to make contact with any of his family?"

"So far, only a grandfather."

Laine perked up. "In Miami?"

"In a nursing home. Dementia."

Laine slumped back against the counter.

"Admitting is working on it, Laine."

"That young man has one foot in heaven. His family needs to be here with him—if only to say good-bye... if that's what it comes to. Tell Admitting to work faster."

Chapter 6

On the morning of October 23, 2009—what should have been a morning as typically beautiful and leisurely and, yes, *exciting* as any other for a high-flying, well-to-do American expat money launderer living in a tropical paradise—I found myself attempting a frame of mind in which I could comfortably contemplate what might happen to me if I pissed off sixteen Mexican drug lords.

Even drug lords as elegant and erudite as mine had their limits.

I *was* living in paradise. Glorious as the Bahamas are, to say that when I'd woken up that morning I'd had even the most minor intention of ending my day there would have been a serious stretch. Between my gorgeous, lovingly restored colonial mansion in the heart of the Yucatan's White City, and the condo I'd purchased in Miami, the living room of which offered an astonishing view of Biscayne Bay, a small but dazzling pied-a-terre that made my frequent business trips to Florida much more pleasant than even the grandest hotel could have managed—I'd found my home, and put down my roots.

Still, there I was, on my business partner Pablo's private jet, which he was too generous about putting at my disposal; he was so unstinting, in fact, I had yet to purchase my own wings, though it was certainly an item on my to-do list. There I was, making an emergency trip to Freeport as dawn was breaking over the Yucatan skyline.

Jack was already in Freeport. He'd grabbed the first commercial flight he could book the day before, as soon as he'd hung up on his mother's summoning phone call. Once he got there it had taken him less than a minute in the hospital room, assessing his father's condition, for him to decide that I needed to be there too. I'd called Pablo to borrow his plane, had Pedro throw a few things in a duffle bag while I took a quick shower, and was in the air in under an hour. Now, though I'd phoned him when we had taken off only to give him an estimated ETA, Jack seemed reluctant to end our call. "Have the steward bring you breakfast on the plane," he said. "The breakfast pickings are sparse in the cafeteria here, an orange or a banana, a day-old Danish or an airport muffin, and the coffee sucks..."

"Jack?" In response, he took another drag of the cigarette he was sucking on while he paced the few yards that made up the hospital's outdoor smoking area. "I think you're avoiding going back to your father's hospital room."

"My father has a tube down his throat so he can't talk and he's the color of caulking paste—

and my mother! She's holding his hand, sitting so ramrod straight in a chair by his bed you could use her as a right angle. Of course I'm avoiding going back in there."

David and Candace are Jack's parents and, I could say truly in all respects except actual blood, they are mine as well. They'd been on what we all cheerfully referred to as a "vacation" in Freeport but really they were living there, on an extended holiday of indeterminate length designed to keep them away from the harsh spotlight and out of the boiling media pressure cooker as their elder blood son, Abe, was arrested, arraigned, and stood trial for embezzling two million dollars from the family bank.

The trial had been over for six months. Abe was behind bars, barely one-sixteenth into his eight-year sentence—not counting time off for good behavior—Thanksgiving was approaching, and Jack had begun hinting to his mom and dad that he'd really like it if they were home for the holidays. He'd had the staff at their Spanish-style estate outside of Homestead do a thorough, top-to-bottom cleaning so their house would sparkle when they arrived, stopped by to see that the gardeners had maintained Candace's climbing roses in bright profusion over the wide front entry, exactly as she liked them, and restocked the bar with David's favorite single malts—all in anticipation of the homecoming. And yet he could not get his parents to commit to a return date.

"They just aren't up to coming home yet," I'd said, part of my campaign to get Jack to stop pestering them and let them move forward on their own terms and in their own time. Lord knew that I'd always been the sort to push back hard when people tried to force me to do what they thought was good for me; Jack's pestering *me* hadn't ever been helpful. Moreover, I thought Jack was being a little insensitive to the magnitude of his brother's betrayal of the family trust, perfidy that had hit his parents hard, David particularly. He's always kept himself in great shape, playing rigorous tennis two or three times a week, and, though he's bald and a little wrinkled around the edges, he'd always carried himself with both vigor and dignity. In May, however, in the twenty-four hours that had elapsed between Abe's crime coming to light and his arrest, David had aged twenty years.

Now David was in a hospital in Freeport with a tube down his throat.

"He's had episodes before," Jack confided to me from his smoking-zone haunt. "His doctor down here categorized them as panic attacks, but this ... This is not a panic attack. This is... Clint, the doctor was tossing around the word 'stroke' like it was a fucking football. He wants to do more tests before he commits to a diagnosis, you know, they always want to do more tests... I don't know— maybe you're right, I pushed too hard for him and Mom to come back to Florida and he just couldn't take it—"

"Oh, for fuck's sake, *Jack*." I was pleased that Jack had lately started to take on responsibility and to deal with what he put on his plate, like a reasonable adult. In the time since Abe's arrest he had stepped up at the bank, into his father's large shoes, and, with me as his partner, completely turned it around. We had transformed a small family operation that had been on the FDIC watch list into a thriving institution with an ever-growing number of branches. I was beginning to understand, however, that responsibility was something you didn't just step into, as Jack had, at thirty-four years of age. It was something you had to cultivate throughout your life if you were to learn how to apportion it in any way appropriately. Now Jack was taking responsibility for even those things that were out of his control—like his father's suspected stroke.

"Jack?"

Still, he said nothing.

And then I heard him sob.

For both Jack and me, the potential loss of David—his father and the only father figure I'd ever known—was devastating to even consider. I had the horrible thought—a morbid version of fuck/marry/kill—that I didn't know which would be worse: David dead or David so profoundly disabled he couldn't play tennis or drink Scotch or crack a joke, or maybe even recognize any of his sons, blood or otherwise, and I knew I had to banish it.

So I thought about Pablo, the emperor among my roster of south-of-the-border kingpins. David, the president and chairman of the board of the American bank that laundered all of their money might just have had a stroke. What was that going to mean for our laundry business? How nervous was it going to make my temperamental customers? Jack and I were good at our jobs, efficient and personable and honest and creative, but David was the one with all the connections at the Fed; his long-standing friendships with the people who do—or who do *not* do—the auditing were key to our business's success. Jack and I were only beginning to cultivate our own relationships with David's cronies, only beginning to earn their trust. The fact that David introduced both of us as his sons—vouching for us as cut from his same cloth—gave us only slight credibility in that crowd. David knew it, we knew it, and Pablo and his cohorts knew it. Abe's arrest, not to mention the subsequent publicity of the trial, had set the kingpins on edge. The spotlight of the trial, law enforcement breathing down everyone's neck: these were situations that displeased the kingpins. To put it mildly. I'd earned every fucking penny of my cut in the months until Abe was safely behind bars, babysitting the kingpins whose temperaments careened collectively, in those unsettling times, between pitifully disappointed CEOs and a pack of two-year-olds on a murderous rampage. The loss of David—his ability to pick up a phone even from the Bahamian surfside and smooth our path with just one call—was going to put them on another edge entirely. This was a place, naturally, I did not want them to go—and, I worried, with or without my news, Pablo was already headed there.

My kingpins were not secretive with me—to the contrary. I'd been to Pablo's plush bunker on numerous occasions, among gatherings from across the Mexican nation, and not once had I experienced that awkward sensation of having a conversation come to a screeching halt because I'd entered into it. And so I'd learned a great deal over the previous months about how the cartels operated—or, I had at least learned those things that I needed to know in order to operate my small part of their business most efficiently. I was well aware that there was much I still did not know, that was being discreetly kept from me, and I sensed that the gaps that existed in my knowledge were purposeful, for my own protection. *If I told you, then I'd have to kill you.* I am curious by nature, but I do not have a death wish.

Even so, it wouldn't have stretched the imagination of even a person without my nearly preternatural people-reading skills to know that something was off in Cartel World these days. Within the last month or so, Pablo, under normal circumstances the most hospitable of men, had stopped issuing his nearly weekly invitations to dine at his hacienda. Our daily phone calls had ceased to contain any semblance of their usual banter; Pablo got right down to business and hung up as immediately as it was concluded. Most ominously, he'd assigned an additional four armed guards to ride on the armored cars for pick-up and deliveries to Reforma. That last, alone, would have been enough to make me ask questions if I were a stupid man.

These are the thoughts I clung to as Pablo's plane whisked me into the starkly beautiful Caribbean sunrise, while Jack sobbed, so I wouldn't start sobbing myself.

Chapter 7

"**I**'M only going to say this one more time, Laine," Aletha called into Eddie Collier's room, as she filed her charts and packed up her purse at the end of her shift, "you need to get yourself home." Then, more gently, walking softly into the room herself and placing a professional hand on Laine's shoulder, "You can't do anything more for him now. You need to let the day shift nurses look after him."

Laine looked around, at the eleven other pie-shaped cubicles that surrounded the nurse's station in the ICU. Only one was empty, without a dying human being in its bed, but in every other one the patient was attended by at least one family member. A grown child praying for his mother, a loving spouse holding the hand of her beloved in silent vigil. In the cubicle directly across the room a teenager stood by her grandfather's bed and sang, softly, again and over again, in a surprisingly sure alto, the old man's favorite hymn. "Be Thou my vision, O Lord of my heart..."

"There's nobody here for this young man," Laine explained. "I can't leave him all alone. I mean, we don't even know his name—"

"No, Laine, we do know his name. It's Edward, remember?'

"Edward, sure, on his driver's license. But do his friends call him Ed? Did his mom call him Eddie? Maybe he goes by his middle name... Maybe he's Jimmy..."

Aletha sighed. She was in her early fifties, too far from retirement to be so exhausted at the end of her twelve-hour shift, aching to get home and sit down with a glass of wine, spend some time with her oldest daughter who was due home for a week-long break from Florida State. But she knew as well as anyone else on the floor that Eddie wasn't expected to make it through the day. She'd read his chart. She'd noted the subtle indications of systems shut-down on its pages herself. She was aware that the most Christian act anyone could perform for Eddie Collier at this point in his short life was to direct that the intubation tube currently down his throat be removed so he could die in peace, and quickly—and that the only person besides his doctor who could authorize the removal was an old man in a nursing home suffering from profound senile dementia.

"Ham and cheese or chicken salad?" Aletha asked, tossing her purse onto the one empty visitor's chair in Eddie's cubicle.

Laine looked up at her.

"You have to eat. Let's get something in your stomach..."—she rummaged in her purse for her wallet—"I'm making a cafeteria run—what do you want?"

Aletha's question, at first, made Laine feel the grip of panic in her chest; she knew she wasn't yet prepared to make that hard call about Eddie's intubation. But she also knew that it was a decision kindness required of her. And that the nurse had just offered to stay with her while it was done.

"Chicken salad," Laine said.

Chapter 8

Jack met me at the main entrance to the Rand Memorial Hospital in Freeport, an unlit cigarette dangling from the fingers of his left hand and his cell phone clutched in his right as he fumbled to help me out of the cab I'd taken from the airport.

"I've got it. I've got it," I told him to get him to let go of the duffle bag I was trying to sling over my own shoulder. I defaulted into irritation at him, rather than face my deep unease about David, and we both knew what I was doing. "Just walk me over to the smoking area where you can light that fucking thing and tell me what's going on."

Jack's hands shook as he lit his cigarette. "Dad's awake," he said as he exhaled, his voice strangled by emotion and smoke.

"Jack! That's great—"

Jack's head moved furiously, nodding yes and shaking no at the same time, and he spoke at the same furious speed. "He's awake, his doctor is in with him now, taking the intubation tube out, the nurses shooed Mom and me out of the room while the doctor did the procedure but he doesn't have any idea what Dad's going to be like when he can talk to us again. Is he going to be able to talk? Is he going to be able to walk? Is he going to know where he is and who we are? If it was all good news I had to tell you, you think I wouldn't have spit it out the minute you got out of the cab?"

I actually rocked back on my feet with the force of Jack's words, and I had to reach out to steady myself on the enormous red plastic ash chimney into which Jack was flicking his cigarette. "Shouldn't we go inside and find your mom? Shouldn't we be with her—she shouldn't be alone ..."

Jack shook his head. "We have twenty minutes. At least. Dad's nurse said she'd come and find us when the procedure was done, and Mom is elated. Rejoicing. In total denial. She's got this idea in her head that, now that he's awake, Dad's going to be his old self again. She's in the powder room now, fixing her makeup, so she looks her best for him. You know Mom—the classic iron hand in a designer velvet glove." He shrugged as he stubbed out his cigarette on the side of the red plastic container. "It's not like her to be so willfully unrealistic."

I nodded. Jack may have thought of his mom as an iron hand in an expensive velvet glove; my own metaphor revolved more around a beautifully manicured hand that, no matter how often we boys—David, Jack, me, and even Abe—disappointed her, still held us tightly; we were balloons and it was Candace who held tenaciously onto the strings that kept us from floating off into the ether. We could take as many risks as we dared because

Candace always had her feet on the ground. If Candace was becoming untethered I didn't know where that would leave us.

But it was Candace who'd always advised us to face the worst head-on. "*Potato chips*? You *stole* potato chips? I'm not having you boys turn into petty thieves," she'd scolded as she marched us back into the convenience store to confess our sin to the acned teenage manager when we were ten years old. "You two were the ones who wrecked his car, you two are the ones who need to tell him what you did," she'd told us when we were teenagers, after we'd "borrowed" David's Cadillac and run it into a ditch on the side of Krome Avenue. "You put your shoulders back and hold your head up high, Clint. Don't take any shit and you'll get through this," she'd said to me when I was in my twenties, right before I surrendered myself to begin a jail sentence for running an escort service. I hadn't turned into a petty thief; I'd turned into a pimp and, still, Candace had my back.

"Let's go do this," I said to Jack, jerking my head in the general direction of David's hospital room.

He stuffed the butt down the small opening at the top of the red chimney and replied. "Let's go."

Chapter 9

LAINE felt Aletha's hand on her back, rubbing her gently but firmly between her tensed shoulder blades. It was comfort she appreciated. She held one of Eddie's hands in both of hers and she didn't want to transfer the fury inside of her to her patient. Why was no one here for this mortally injured young man!

The new charge nurse on duty drew back the curtain around Eddie's bed to whisper, "Laine, we can handle it from here. Why don't you two head on home?"

Laine shook her head. "There's no one else here for him." She let out a snicker. "As it stands"—she looked around the room, at her two companions—"I'm his oldest friend right now." She shook her head again. "But you have to go home, Aletha. You've gone above and beyond as it is—"

Aletha responded by rubbing Laine's shoulders a little more firmly; she wasn't going anywhere.

Laine nodded. "Any luck getting hold of that guy?" she asked the charge nurse. "The guy the nursing home told us about, who takes over as guardian for Edward's grandfather in case something happens to Edward?"

The charge nurse sighed. "Clint Kennedy. As far as admin can figure out, he lives primarily in Mexico these days. They're still trying to track down a cell phone number for him."

"Jesus Christ," Laine muttered under her breath.

Chapter 10

DAVID was in a private room on the third floor at Ryder. Jack and I walked in, Candace between us, an arm braced on each of us. David turned from the nurse who stood over his head, wiping spittle from his chin with a warm cloth, and cocked his head at us. He gave us a smile that was both broad and lopsided. "Ha-ah!" he attempted to bellow in greeting, but he coughed, so he waved at us with his left hand, which I thought was odd as I knew he was right-handed. I turned to Jack, silently corroborating with him that my assessment of the situation wasn't as rosy as Candace's, but there were tears standing in his eyes and I had to look away.

"Thank you," David said to his nurse, enunciating painfully, the 'th' sounding thick, as if he were saying 'tank'.

"Mr. Cohen, let's not try to speak just yet," the nurse urged.

David gently pushed her warning and her ministering hand away with his good arm. His next request, "Come here," was directed at the three

of us and more easily understood than his gratitude to the nurse. We did as we were commanded,
and David allowed a full two or three minutes for
us to greet him and tell him how happy we were
to see him, and how glad we were that he was
awake, and enthuse wasn't he looking better already, before he grew restless. He tried to talk to
us, but speaking was painful, and forming words
frustrated him, and he waved his good hand at the
table near his bed. I saw the notepad and pencil
the nurse had placed there and quickly moved the
pad so he could reach it and placed the pencil in
his fist. His scribbles were almost as hard to de-
cipher as his speech—a not entirely upsetting development considering he was trying to write with
his left hand—but Candace and Jack and I were
quick to jump in and guess the words before he
had to write out each one. "J" we guessed cor-
rectly meant Jack, and "C" meant Candace, and
'g' meant get or go, and so on, until we understood his desire: Jack was to take Candace to
their apartment in Freeport and bring back his
toothbrush and his eyeglasses; he would be fine
because I would stay with him. Which, of course,
I was glad to do, but as soon as Jack and Candace
had cleared the door on their way to do David's errands, he waved the nurse out of the room too and
caught the tail of my shirt in his hand and pulled
me until I was bent over the bed, close enough to
him that he could hiss in my ear, slowly but un-
mistakably: "Get me the fuck out of here." Then
he started to cough again.

I picked up the plastic cup of water on his bedtable and held the straw while he sipped.

The look of relief that spread over his face as he took in the water was heartbreaking. His next words came slowly and deliberately, but with complete conviction: Candace and Jack wanted him to stay in the hospital, in Freeport, until his doctor down here thought he was sufficiently recovered to go home.

"That seems like a good idea to me—"

David thumped the bed with his good hand and coughed out, "Don't be a moo-rah!"

It took me a minute to catch up. "Moron? I shouldn't be a moron?"

David cackled, in spite of himself, and gripped the pencil, scrawling an 'X' on the pad.

"Ummm...?"

He retraced the 'X' with some irritation.

"Ah! Xavier? You want to see Xavier?"

He nodded happily and scribbled a 'w', followed by an 'i' and an 'l', nearly spelling out the entire word before I understood he wanted me to say 'will'.

I immediately tried to change the subject. "Can't all that sort of thing wait until you're feeling better?" I asked.

David's reply came as clear as I would hear him speak for several months, not until after he'd completed eight weeks of grueling speech therapy: "What if I die before I get better?" he demanded. The effort sent him to a spasm of coughs and the nurse scurrying back into the room.

"Mr. Kennedy," she snapped at me, "he shouldn't be talking! I think it will be good if you have a seat in the waiting room until the Cohens get back if you insist on conversing with him."

Chapter 11

THE tires of Jessie Coulter's custom-red BMW Gran Turismo bumped hard over a pothole in the parking lot of the strip mall where his office was located. "Goddamn it," he growled, low. He always intended to steer around that pothole, the biggest of the hazards that pock-marked the lot, though he frequently failed to actually do it. Often that was because he was on the phone as he pulled in off busy West Okeechobee Road, growling loudly into the speaker on behalf of one client or another, gesturing wildly as if the person on the other end of his cell could actually see him, distracted by his own bluster. Jessie thought of himself as a hard-assed negotiator. In reality he was a cut-rate attorney the more mainstream attorneys in Dade County dreaded having to deal with, not because he was an intimidating adversary, but because he was unreasonable in his own arrogance. Attorneys like Xavier Sousa didn't even know who he was.

But Judge Kushner knew who he was, and that was all that mattered to Jessie. Jessie's clients were primarily—if not exclusively—elderly folks whose estates were in conservatorships, and Kushner—nearly exclusively—reviewed the court filings for those who were served by court-appointed public guardians. As long as Kushner got his weekly cash for throwing business Jessie's way, new clients would keep rolling into Jessie's practice.

Today Jessie missed steering around the pothole because he was doing forty in the parking lot, trying to keep himself under fifteen minutes late for his first meeting of the day. He hated it when Carla, his secretary, scheduled meetings for him before nine AM, but what were you going to do? Someone wanted to give you money, but you had to get to your office at the crack of dawn in order to put it in your pocket? Jessie was fine setting the alarm a little earlier to make his bank balance a little fatter. He was flexible like that.

Chapter 12

I stood outside of the main entrance to Rand Memorial, holding my cell phone in my hand. There were several messages from a number I didn't recognize, but nothing from Tim and that was comforting: it meant that the day's transfers were being handled without incident. Pablo was going to have enough reasons to be jacked and it was nice to know that a fuck-up involving his money wasn't going to be one of them.

"How is Miami!" Pablo asked by way of greeting when he picked up.

That was the level of trust between Pablo and me: he hadn't even asked where I was going with his plane. He'd simply assumed that Miami, as it so often was, was my destination.

"I'm in Freeport, Pablo."

It is a testament to how quickly Pablo's agile mind worked that the next words out of his mouth were, "How are David and Candace?" though he'd never actually met either of them.

I took a breath before I spoke. "David's in the hospital, Pablo. He's had a stroke—a very minor one," I hastened to add even if I wasn't sure at this point how much of a lie that was. When there wasn't a response from Pablo's end I continued. "He wants to go back to Miami, sleep in his own bed, have his own doctors looking after him, all that, you understand. I'd like to take him there this afternoon. On your plane. You're always so generous, and I was pretty sure you'd be all right with that, but I didn't want to presume..."

Pablo was still silent.

I waited him out.

"I know you have a great deal of affection for David Cohen, and I'm sorry for this trouble, Clint. Call me when you arrive in Miami. So I know you have all arrived. Safely."

I didn't realize I'd been holding my breath until I exhaled.

There are two kinds of criminals in the world— good criminals and bad criminals. I am a good criminal. A good criminal owns his illegal livelihood. He doesn't try to hide his crimes behind laws enacted by venal politicians and intended to screw the public; he doesn't do business primarily on busy streets—K Street... Wall Street. I mean, I hide what I do from law enforcement, of course, but I make no excuses for it. People get killed in my line of work—not by me; and I've made my peace with the reality that if anyone is stupid enough to cross the head of a cartel, maybe he doesn't deserve to live—but, hey, there's an upside too. Good criminals look after their own.

For the most part.

"I might have to be in Miami for a few days, Pablo," I ventured, and added, "I trust Tim to handle things while I'm out of town."

Pablo replied once again with that menacing silence. Then he said, "I think, Clint, it is better that you are out of town for the next few days, in any case."

What the hell did that mean? I stared at my phone but Pablo, as had lately become his habit, had disconnected abruptly as soon as he'd had his say. I might have simply kept staring, my curiosity getting in the way of my better senses, but I saw the ambulance pull around to the entrance—the vehicle that was being used to transport David to the airfield where we would all board Pablo's plane to Miami—and I expected the Cohens, Jack and Candace and David in a wheelchair pushed by the nurse they'd hired to make the trip to the US with us, to come filing off the elevator at any moment. And then my phone began to ring. The mystery number from earlier in the day flashed on the screen.

"What?" I barked.

"Ah, umm, yes, I've been trying hard to reach a Mr. Clint Kennedy. Is that who I'm speaking to?" A female voice of indeterminate age but with a hard, mid-Western accent greeted me.

"Who's calling?"

"I'm calling from Ryder Trauma Center, on behalf of one of our patients, Mr. Edward James Collier..."

Chapter 13

"**Y**ou fucking criminal!"

Jessie heard Carla gasp as he ducked around his desk, away from the middle-aged woman who had passed herself off as his new client. The woman wouldn't have made him turn his head on the street—she looked like any other middle-class Miami retiree in her pastel, cropped-leg pants and espadrilles, with her laying-in-the-sand-drinking-Margaritas-all-day girth, sporting a dyed-blonde hairstyle that she clearly hadn't changed since she was in her 1980s heyday. But there was no question she had no medical need for the cane she'd hobbled in on, and Jessie, for his part, had to give her props for devising such a convincing way in which to get a weapon into his office.

"Ma'am," he soothed as he held his cocoa-brown desk chair between himself and the desk the woman was now clearing with the tip of the red-and-silver candy-cane-striped weapon. Sheaves of paper flew out of manila folders, the black plastic desktop phone went flying into a window on the far side of the office, making the jointed skeleton hanging there dance and cracking a pane of glass.

And then the glass jar of Jelly Belly jellybeans—a personal addiction since the Reagan administration—shattered on the scuffed hardwood floor.

"Don't you 'ma'am' me!" the woman screeched, cane flailing, "that's my great-aunt you're ripping off, you crook!"

"Who?" Jessie pleaded, keeping one eye on the woman and one eye on the cane she was wielding erratically, and too near his head. "Your great-aunt who?"

"Ethel Nestor!" the woman screamed. "Ethel Nestor! The old woman you moved out of her perfectly lovely nursing home in Miami Beach and into some dump in Homestead!"

Jessie had no idea which of his clients the crazy woman was talking about, but he had a pat answer for disgruntled relatives: "I had to move her! It's my job to make sure these old people have enough money to last the rest of their lives—it would be irresponsible of me to leave her in a high-priced facility only to see her run out of money-"

Wham! The woman stretched her arm above her head and brought her menacing cane down on the top of Jessie's desk. "Aunt Ethel is ninety-three and she's worth seven million dollars! Just how do you see her running out of money!"

Aha, Jessie thought. He knew exactly who the lunatic was talking about now. Ethel Nestor was a relatively new client but certainly one of his more lucrative ones. Between the kickbacks from Sunset Gardens Elder Care and the conservatorship fees Judge Kushner approved for him, Jessie wouldn't need to bring in another new client as long as old Ethel remained alive and kicking.

"What do you have to say for yourself, you thief!" The woman screamed, whirling her cane several times over her head before smashing it into the front of the metal desk.

Except for worrying about where the woman was going to aim her cane next, this was another easy question. "I have a legal responsibility to make sure that the interests of the client's heirs are considered—" Even if this wasn't true by any stretch of the imagination, it was often a sentiment that soothed relatives who were due to inherit. It moved them from thinking about the physical comfort of their loved ones to thinking about the vacations they'd be able to take or the fishing boat they'd be able to buy with the money he saved for them on nursing home care.

"Wrong answer, asshole!" the woman shrieked and rushed the desk, heading right so that when Jessie ducked out from behind his chair, on the left, he thought he had a good chance of escaping out the door to the reception area where Carla stood, trembling, bringing the violence before a witness's eyes, but the woman had faked him out. She doubled back and he ran right into her. The look on her face—a perverted, evil glee—as she brought her cane down on him, scared him more than the whoosh the cane made as it sliced the air and connected with his knee.

Chapter 14

WHAT was wrong with me? Why were these delicious jolts of adrenaline continuing to course through my body? Why did I always experience this intense sort of pleasure only when things stood a good chance of going wrong?

I flipped on the light in the entry way to my condo and barely made it to the sofa before I collapsed. The day had been backbreaking—especially coming on top of having pulled an all-nighter at my school. I thought I should probably call Miguel and explain the changes I'd left on the library drawings, not to mention why the drawings were strewn all over our shared desk, but it was evening now, and he'd likely already left for the day. Besides, I was exhausted. There wasn't an ounce of me that had the will to spend one more minute in logical thought. But—there it was again —just when I thought all I wanted was something to eat and my bed, another electric jolt, this one possibly because I realized I hadn't called ahead to have the condo prepared for me. There was no food in the house, and I wasn't sure the bed was made up. *Fuck.*

I sprawled on the sofa, looking out over the lights on Biscayne Bay, deciding what I was going to do about my predicament. Pour a couple of fingers of the vodka that was certainly still ice cold in the freezer and make a meal out of the cocktail olives? Take myself out for a quick meal at a restaurant? Drag my ass to the bedroom and throw some sheets on the bed, send myself to sleep without dinner, put the day behind me and just start over in the morning? I got as far as getting fresh sheets on the bed.

Then I gave up and called Xavier.

He showed up in less than an hour bearing a twelve-pack of cold Heineken and a large, steaming hot pepperoni pizza.

"Slumming?" I asked him when I opened the door to him.

"As I get older, I find myself becoming less rigid," he answered, grinning at me.

"Apparently to a remarkable degree." I grinned back at him and took the pizza to the kitchen. Xavier followed, popped two of the Heinekens and handed one to me. I leaned against the counter and sipped. Xavier, my friend, attorney, former lover, one-time mentor looked as appealing as he ever had, in spite of the years he had on me, all tall and lean and polished. My attraction to him had never quite completely dissipated—and, I knew, he experienced the same magnetic pull whenever we were together. But, I reminded myself, there were good reasons we'd split. One of them had been his inflexibility—his almost petulant refusal to order in a pizza when that was what I wanted for dinner, instead dragging me out yet again for his favorite French cuisine. If a restaurant didn't have white tablecloths, snails on the menu, and a thirty-page wine list, Xavier didn't want to go inside. I took another sip of my beer and wondered if this meal wasn't a sort of a come-on. Xavier leaned on the opposite counter and drank his own beer. I wanted to laugh, watching him lift the bottle to his mouth, a sight I thought I'd never see.

"David's settled?"

I nodded. "His doctor arranged for a nurse to stay for the night, until he and Candace can arrange for around-the-clock care tomorrow. He's tired, but he's really happy to be home. He wants you to stop by as soon as humanly possible—he's undone about the state of his will..."

Xavier looked at me over the top of his beer bottle.

"What?"

Xavier shrugged. "Just thinking that it isn't unusual for a person who's been through the sort of health scare he's just had to want to get his affairs in order."

I squinted at Xavier. Though I supposed what he'd said was true, it felt as if there was something else he wasn't spitting out.

"How did it go at the hospital? With Eddie?" he asked.

The man didn't miss a beat. Helping Eddie die had, without question, been the most devastating part of a trying day. I hadn't seen the kid in years, but holding his hand while he laid in that hospital bed and took his last breath had nearly done *me* in. I felt my eyeballs start to leak and I really didn't want to do that in front of Xavier. "Years ago"—I lifted my arm to wipe at my cheeks with my sleeve—"I signed some paperwork for Eddie. I agreed to be his grandfather's guardian if something happened to him. I never thought I'd have to live up to that agreement—Eddie was younger than I am, you know? I'll dig the paperwork out of my files and I'd appreciate it if you'd look it over for me."

"Of course."

All I could do was nod as I grabbed a yard or so of paper toweling and turned my back so I could wipe my eyes again and blow my nose.

"The funny part"—I spoke quickly, to cover for my tears—"is that, at the hospital, I met Eddie's surgeon. Laine Gordon. That's her name. Cute blonde. And she stayed with Eddie even though she didn't have to do that, until the hospital could locate a next-of-kin. Or, you know, until they could track me down. And"—I turned back around and laughed because it seemed an appropriate way of dealing with the reaction I'd had to the woman; making fun of myself—"I got so *horny*. Just, this woman, I mean, cute and blonde and all, and maybe my type when it comes to women, but the *intensity* of the lust. You know, I'm watching someone die and I just got all kinds of worked up..."

Xavier smiled. "That's not unusual," he said.

I squinted at him again.

"In the face of death, doing something that's life-affirming can become imperative. What's more life-affirming than making love?"

And there it was again, that incredible, electric jolt.

I don't actually remember moving my feet to make my way across the kitchen. All I remember is falling into Xavier's arms.

We affirmed life for several hours.

Chapter 15

Jessie sat at his metal desk, his leg propped up, heel resting on an overturned trash basket, an ice pack Carla had made for him resting on his swollen knee. Carla had spent most of the day on her hands and knees, crawling around the office floor, picking her way through the rubble of shattered glass and jelly beans, scooping up and trying to reorganize the papers the crazy woman —Leonora Nestor Lingham, great-niece of the not-yet-deceased Ethel Nestor—had flung from the file cabinets and strewn across every surface in the office. Once Jessie had been incapacitated, clutching his knee and moaning on the floor beneath his desk, and with Carla still cowering in the reception area, Christ, had Leonora made a mess. And she hadn't done it methodically, as if she was searching for something, like her great-aunt's file; she had done it with the sole intent of creating chaos of Jessie's more-or-less orderly filing system. It was at least as orderly as any other paper-filing system, Jessie figured; he understood his methods but anyone who might come in to audit it would be suitably confused. With

a paper system, he could create plausible denia-
bility when necessary, and even shred files if the
circumstances required it. He wanted nothing to
do with computers; their memories were far too
long and precise and indisputable.

Carla huffed and handed Jessie another stack of
papers. Crawling around on the floor was hard for
her—she'd been rather substantially overweight
for most of her sixty-odd years and her knees were
in no shape for the sort of athletics this sort of
exercise required. Jessie's knee, however, was
in even worse shape. She winced again as she
glanced at it, swollen to almost twice its normal
size.

"Should I have called the police?" Carla asked.

"Hell, Carla," Jessie replied, leafing through the
sheaf Carla had just handed him, "you never call
the police." He laughed. "Unless there's a dead
body, you know, and even then... You don't ever
want the police all up in your business. You did
just what I told you to do when something like this
happens: you hid and let me deal with it. Here."
Jessie ripped the cardboard cover from one of the
composition notebooks he used to code and tally
his weekly payouts. "There's some duct tape in
the top drawer of the credenza—put this over the
window until I can get the landlord to get off his
lazy ass and replace the pane."

Making what Jessie referred to as "free money"
—taking a hefty fee for administering the estates
of people who, for one reason or another, had
been declared wards of the state—wasn't without

its hazards. Jessie grunted and repositioned his wounded knee. Cost of doing business.

"But"—Carla cleared her throat—"your knee..." Which she did find alarming, how it had ballooned and was straining the fabric of Jessie's wrinkled khaki trousers, though her primary concern in all of this was her box of trinkets. In her rampage, Leonora Nestor Lingham had made it to the drawers of Carla's desk and upturned the cardboard box decorated with decoupaged Christmas trees that Carla kept in the lower left drawer. The woman had really had to work to dislodge that box, tucked as Carla always kept it behind the first aid kit and other junk in that drawer. In the box, Carla kept the treasures from her adventures: the baby-blue pacifier she'd surreptitiously urged off a stroller at the park while the baby was asleep and she was distracting the young mother with lively conversation; the five sets of silverware— fork, spoon and butter knife—she'd procured, one utensil at a time, during her weekly lunches at Applebee's. She loved their boneless ribs and with just one more set, she'd have service for six. There was also the Dunhill lighter she had acquired from Judge Errol Kushner's office one day, years before, when she went to see his secretary, Barbara, to file a bunch of POAs. The lighter was engraved with the judge's initials—EK; "Eeeek!" she giggled whenever she took it out to admire it, such silly initials for a man as distinguished as the judge. The treasures were now strewn all over the floor under her desk chair. She couldn't have Jessie wandering to her outer office and wondering what all of those shiny things were and how she came into possession of them. Some of the trinkets had once belonged to him! She felt guiltily grateful that Jessie was too injured to do much wandering and, still, she thought he ought to have someone who knew about such things see to that knee. "Don't you think we ought to get you to an emergency room?"

Jessie's reply startled her—an "Aha!" so fierce it was almost accusatory and caused her to juggle the Dunhill lighter and drop it to the floor. Jessie gripped a blue-covered bundle of legal-sized papers and waved it over his head. "Here it is!"

"What is?" Carla dropped to her knees to scout for the lost treasure.

"That Nestor broad's will." Jessie rifled through the sheets, folding the pages back on one another. "Ha!" he cackled when he found what he was looking for. "The Nestor broad, her beneficiary is the Animal Rights Foundation of Florida!"

"Why is that important?" she asked, rolling her chair out of the way and peering under desk for the missing trinket.

Jessie rolled his eyes. "The niece isn't in line to inherit a goddamned thing. She has no standing, telling me which nursing home to park her aunt. What the fuck's her problem?"

Carla nodded, thinking. Maybe it had bounced behind the filing cabinet? "Maybe she just wants her aunt to live out what's left of her life in comfort?"

Jessie rested the will on his lap and took a moment to think about that. Finally, he shrugged.

"Yeah, I s'pose that could be," he said. "Anything's possible."

Chapter 16

Saturday, October 24, 2009

LATE the next morning, we were grouped around the breakfast table in the Cohen's spacious kitchen—Candace and Jack on the settee, Xavier and me on two matching wrought iron chairs, and David pushed tight into the table in his wheelchair. His nurse bent to wipe his mouth before she left us to have our meeting in privacy. David indulged her, grudgingly. It was his right side that had been affected by his stroke; he was going to need physical therapy to get his right leg back in gear so he could walk, and to regain control of his right arm. Speech therapy would help him speak properly again, and work his facial muscles so spittle no longer collected at the corner of his mouth and rolled down his chin. David was maintaining his dignity, even while sitting among us in his pajamas and a robe, but it was clear by the way he sat rigid and annoyed while the nurse wiped his chin, that the drooling was mortifying for him. Candace placed a clean white napkin in his good left hand so he'd at least have the means to clean up his own spit.

Candace served cups of piping hot dark roast, and Xavier took the lead in getting the meeting started. "David asked us all to gather here this morning to go over a few concerns his recent health scare have brought to light." He stirred a teaspoon of sugar into his coffee before he continued. "The most pressing is that, due to his conviction for embezzlement, and according to the terms of his sentence, Abe is no longer allowed to own shares in any financial institution. The formality of having Abe sign his existing shares back to his father has never been addressed."

Jack's eyes narrowed. "So, what does that mean? Someone's got to go see him in jail and have him sign off on the paperwork?"

"That's what's required," Xavier confirmed.

Jack smiled. "I'll go."

I shook my head, and Candace actually gasped. "You just want to go to rub your brother's nose in it," she said to her son.

"Yes," Jack agreed happily. "Clint will go with me."

"Well, that will thrill Abe," David observed, not without humor, and though his diction was off, we all got the joke.

"Let's work toward a peaceable solution," Xavier said and then snickered as he pushed a manila envelope in David's direction. "There are three copies of the document in there. Whoever you decide to send as your emissary—and I'm happy to send someone from my office, if that makes it easier on everyone—make sure that person gets Abe to sign all three." He picked up a second manila envelope and opened it. "David, I made the revisions to your will you asked for when we talked last evening. I think you'll find everything in order, but please take a moment to read it over before you sign."

David accepted the documents from Xavier with his left hand, then placed them on the table in front of him to free his good hand so he could lift the glasses he wore on a chain around his neck to his face. Candace read over his shoulder, and the rest of us sipped our coffees quietly while David perused his updated will.

"Are you happy with this, Candace?" David asked when he had finished reading.

His wife placed her hand on top of his and nodded. David nodded back, and cleared his throat. "I have made some decisions," he told us, speaking slowly to get the most out of his strained enunciation. "And I won't have them questioned," he added, eyeing Jack.

Jack sat up and shook his head, as if fighting his dad on any point would be the last thing he'd consider.

"Good," David said, and, in deference to his current capabilities, motioned to Xavier to continue on his behalf.

"David's estate will go entirely to his wife, Candace," Xavier said, "with two exceptions, a monetary bequest to his son, Abraham, and his stock in the bank, which is to be divided evenly between his son, Jack, and Clint Kennedy."

It was my turn to gasp.

"I will not have this questioned," David added quickly but forcefully.

"It's just... David..." I sputtered, even as I saw Jack smiling, clearly without objection.

Candace lifted her hand from her husband's and placed it on top of mine. "Hush, darling," she whispered to me. "You and Jack are responsible for building the bank to where it is today. It would be absolute heresy if David and I didn't recognize that in these documents. So, you just hush now."

Chapter 17

I stood on the slate patio outside of the Cohen's kitchen, sipping a fresh cup of coffee while Jack smoked a cigarette, trying to pull myself together. I had never had even a thought of being included in David Cohen's will. That I had been, especially in such a generous manner, was a shock. "Are you sure you're OK with this?"

Jack took a long, last draw on his Marlboro before he stubbed it out on the slate. "If you hadn't brought us the Mexican business, there might not *be* a bank for either of us to inherit, bro." He bent to pick up the butt; Candace would never let him hear the end of it if he left it smashed and stinking on her patio. "*Bro*," he repeated, and slapped me on my shoulder before he grabbed me and wrapped me in a hard hug.

"*Bro*," I replied, extracting myself from his embrace. "Don't get all emo on me." I was mortified to see that Jack was coming in for another hug but, before I had to dodge him, I heard the sliding glass door purring in its groove.

"Clint."

I'd never been so happy to see Xavier in my life —and there had been times in my life when I had been ecstatic to see him.

Jack chuckled, and chucked me once more, hard, on my shoulder, before he slipped inside the sliding glass door Xavier had just exited. "How are you this morning?" Xavier asked me.

I knew he wasn't referring to the night we'd just spent together; Xavier was too sophisticated to be coy. "Feeling like I just got knocked on my ass. Again. You knew David was going to do this and you didn't tell me?"

"Wasn't mine to tell," he reminded me. He made his way to the glass-and-wrought-iron table on the Cohen's patio and hoisted his briefcase onto the top of it. "What I *can* tell you is all about Eddie Collier."

"Right." I sank into one of the wrought-iron chairs. I hadn't been in any way particularly close to Eddie—ever; hadn't even seen him, as I've said, in years—and now I wondered if I was ever going to get over standing beside his hospital bed and watching him die. Helping him die.

"The good news," Xavier said, withdrawing the folder of papers I'd handed him when he'd left my condo the night before, "is that Eddie Collier left his grandfather a very rich man."

I looked up at Xavier, unable to hide my skepticism.

"Really. I mean, the pension Elmer gets from all those years of working as a janitor at your old school—he was one of the lucky ones, started out when there were solid union contracts for support workers—from his own assets he could live for ten, fifteen more years and not have to leave the posh nursing home Eddie moved him into when he started making money himself. And Eddie started making *a lot* of money."

I was still frowning. "How? How did Eddie Collier start making so much money..." I shook my head. "How much money are we talking about?"

Xavier shrugged. "Couple million."

"A *couple million*?"

How in the hell had that happened?

"As far as I can tell—and I had only about an hour this morning to delve into the paperwork you gave me and do the most cursory research —but Eddie bought his first house to flip about four years ago. Overall, he lost about three thousand dollars on the deal, which wasn't a lot in any case, for the sort of project he took on but, for him, I think it was money well spent. I mean that, clearly, he was on a fast-paced learning curve because since then he's flipped almost three dozen other houses—mostly single-family homes, bungalows in Coconut Grove he bought in foreclosure —and he's made a nice profit on every one of them, even given the current market."

"But that couldn't account for a couple of million —"

"It could," Xavier explained, "if a guy continued to live frugally and invested the profits in high-risk tech stocks, where the risks, almost universally, paid off handsomely."

'That savvy little shit," I marveled. Eddie must have been paying closer attention to my lectures about fiscal responsibility than I'd thought. "So then why was he still in the escort business? Why did he continue to cultivate the image of an unrepentant party boy?"

Xavier shrugged again. "Maybe he liked the work?"

"Apparently." Eddie's death hadn't gone unnoticed by his former clients. My phone—which I'd silenced during the meeting with the Cohens—was filling up with voicemails and text messages from men who were shocked and grieved at Eddie's passing. Eddie had worked as his own booker since I'd retired from the business and, among the people who were now tracking me down were his long-time and happily satisfied customers. Now that his cell phone was dead in some police evidence bag, I was the only way they knew to get in touch with him.

"There was also a will—the clerk at the courthouse faxed me a copy first thing this morning. I don't know how you'll take this, but you're also Eddie's executor." Xavier paused, to give me a moment to let that sink in. "Not that you're required to take the job—I can always move to have Elmer declared a ward of the state—but I've gathered a few more details for you to mull over as you consider what you're going to do. After Elmer is taken care of—after he passes—Eddie left instructions that the remainder of his assets be donated to the Miami AIDs Project. But who knows how long the old man will be around and, in the meantime, the assets have to be managed. Sell the stocks or reinvest in them, for one thing, but he's also got three flip projects in the works and someone has to make a determination if the renovation work continues on those houses, or if they're sold as is, probably at a loss. That's just for starters..." Xavier added, "As I said, I've been able to do only the most preliminary investigation into just what all of his assets might be."

I felt haunted by my old life. Old johns calling me to find out what happened to their favorite date. Old promises made to a young man about taking care of his grandfather in the unlikely circumstance the old man would outlive him. "I suppose that, being executor, the someone who has to make all these decisions is me?"

"Legally, yeah. That's what you're currently signed up for."

"Shit."

"On the up side," Xavier offered, "you're entitled to a fee for managing the estate, and this is a substantial estate so the fee will be proportional—"

"Oh, Jesus, Xavier, I'm not taking money from an old man. Or the Miami AIDs Project. That's the path to hell."

Xavier laughed. "I never figured you for a religious man, Clint."

"Karma, baby," I replied, and then I had an idea. A brilliant idea. "Xavier!"

"Yes, Clint?"

"Is it part of my management duties to plan Eddie's funeral?"

"It is."

"Then that's what I'm going to spend a little money on."

"Send that boy off in style?"

"That's the plan."

Chapter 18

THE funeral director, whose services I had booked on the recommendation of Laine—she'd used the Fortney-Kline Funeral Home when she'd buried her father over two years before and been quite satisfied with the quality and compassion of their services—didn't know quite what to make of my ideas for Eddie's final send-off. Clearly Laine had made more traditional arrangements for her father.

Mr. Kline wore a beautifully fitted dark-gray suit over a plump frame, and laughably obvious plugs sprouted from his shiny head. I took a seat on a dark-blue upholstered settee in what was designated the "Iris Room" of his sprawling, pristine, Victorian-style set-up. Xavier took the cushion next to me, and Mr. Kline sat across from us in a hard-back chair, both his posture and the way he subtly repositioned a box of tissues nearer to us professional. "I'm so sorry for your loss," he told us, arranging a clipboard on his lap, ballpoint pen at the ready. "Let's talk about Mr. Collier, and the best way we can help you say good-bye."

I was saddened by Eddie's death though we hadn't seen each other in years, and Xavier had never even met him, but I knew exactly the best way to say good-bye to him. "We're going to throw a party for Eddie Collier, Mr. Kline."

Eddie's will had indicated he wanted cremation. I picked out a dark maroon-red cloisonné urn to hold his cremains; the urn would eventually be located in a niche in the memorial wall at the Palm Memorial Cemetery, next to the one Eddie had purchased for the repose of his grandfather's urn, but first it would take place of honor at Club Boi, one of Miami's hottest clubs and Eddie's favorite haunts, at Eddie's going away party. I left Mr. Kline the phone number of Dr. Dack, one of the town's most in-demand d.j.s—he specialized in Hip Hop, Latin, and Old School beats and I knew he was an old friend of Eddie's who would drop any other gig in order to spin for Eddie one last time. As far as food and beverage went, I ordered a full, open bar—with the stipulation that the dozen bartenders I wanted on duty reached only for the top-shelf stuff, and that they did it with their shirts off—and told Mr. Kline that while I wasn't married to any particular restaurant, I wanted a sushi station, a raw bar, and a table with an overflowing spread of Mexican food, Eddie's three favorite ways to eat. As for decorations, I wanted gold streamers glittering under as many disco balls as Club Boi could scare up, gold lame-clad dancers in every cage, and a thousand white balloons dropped from the ceiling at midnight.

Mr. Kline jotted notes furiously, muttering under his breath that he was not a party planner but, when I called him on what I saw as his lack of commitment to my vision—and wondered aloud if another funeral home might be more responsive to the expensive needs of the very wealthy recently deceased—he promised to do the best he could. "No priest, or preacher, or...," was all he added to the conversation.

I had no idea of Eddie's religious preferences, and he'd put nothing in his will that might have given me a clue, but I knew that, among his friends, were a coven of lesbian witches, and I thought I'd ask them to conduct a short service right before the midnight balloon drop.

Mr. Kline sighed heavily, but then quickly assumed his game face again. "Anything else?"

I handed him a thumb drive. Xavier and I had stopped by Eddie's apartment before we'd headed to Fortney-Kline—a two-bedroom, attached townhouse out in Cutler Ridge that was neat and clean, tidily furnished, tastefully accessorized, and completely beneath Eddie's means. It looked as if it had been prepared for a shoot with one of those lower-brow home décor magazines. While we were there I'd downloaded Eddie's entire address book to the thumb drive. "I created an e-vite—you'll find the link on this drive as well—and an invitation should go out to everyone on the list."

Mr. Kline kept a smile on his face, belying the fact that I'd just ruined his entire week, and assured me he'd deliver.

"I think that now would be a good time to do something cheerful," Xavier said as I slumped down Fortney-Kline's front stairs.

"What do you have in mind?" The sun was blazing and I slipped a pair of Ray-Ban Aviators on my face; I was old-school about sunglasses.

Xavier grinned. "Do you think your friend Pablo would mind if we took his plane on a short trip?"

I gave him the side-eye. "To?"

"Savannah."

I love Savannah, Georgia. It's one of my favorite cities, steeped in history and not just a little mystery, awash with gorgeous architecture, delicious Lowcountry cuisine at every turn—she-crab soup and oyster roasts and shrimp and grits... I didn't need much convincing, and still I asked, "What's in Savannah?"

"You'll see," he said, and grinned again.

What I saw, as soon as the plane hit the tarmac at the Savannah/Hilton Head International Airport and we started to descend from Pablo's jet, was a sparkling white Gulfstream G200, ten years old but in pristine condition. "C'mon," Xavier nodded me toward stairs that had been set up to the Gulfstream's door.

The interior was done in cream-colored and pale gray leather, accented with dark navy blue carpet, throw pillows, and over-sized cashmere throws on the backs of two out of the six plush seats. The floor plan included a forward galley, and a rosewood table that lifted hydraulically from the floor; four of the chairs swiveled so a dining or conference area could be set up with the flip of a switch. The configuration also included seating that transformed into single beds at the back of the plane, so the owner and up to four guests could arrive well-rested after longer flights.

"You've been talking about wanting to buy your own plane for a long time now, Clint," Xavier said, sprawling in one of the plush, soft leather seats, "and I think I know why you haven't. Because it can take up to six months for a customized plane to be delivered to you, and your need for immediate gratification is fucking boundless. That is, you'll do without instead of dealing with the wait." He smiled at me, to soften what was seriously the truth about one of my main character flaws. "So —when one of my clients was selling his plane, I asked for photographs." He waved his arms slowly around the cabin. "I thought that it looked like a plane you would design for yourself and so I asked if I could bring you down to Savannah to take a look."

"It's gorgeous, Xavier. How much?"

"Six point nine million."

"And it's really for sale. As is?"

"Write a check and you can fly it away."

I nodded, marveling at the beautiful detailing. Then: "How? How am I supposed to fly it away? I don't have a pilot's license."

"My client's pilot is for hire. You could give him a try, see if it's a good fit. Let him fly you around for a while—you can always fire him if it doesn't work out but, meantime, you buy yourself a little time to search for someone else."

"I'd have to hire a steward..." I mumbled, thinking Pedro would balk at having to add the plane to his housekeeping duties. And that it would be so much more opulent to come through the doors of my very own plane and ask for a vodka martini rather than have to rummage in the galley for ice and olives and alcohol myself.

"Are you trying to talk yourself out of this?" Xavier asked.

I grinned. "Oh, hell, no. Oh, Xavier. Hell, no!"

Xavier and I went to The Olde Pink House for dinner after our shopping spree. We were in the mood to celebrate. We drank champagne, but we couldn't settle on just one entrée each so we shared plates, feasting on Frogmore Stew, Cooter Soup, Hoppin' John, and finished off the meal with two huge slices of Huguenot Torte. We stayed the night at Planters Inn—in separate rooms, which Xavier booked, unrequested, a gesture for which I felt both disappointment and relief, though mostly relief; I had found our recent night together most pleasurable, but I couldn't imagine jumping back fifteen years and trying to have a relationship with him again, notwithstanding that he'd worked past his rigid preoccupation with French cuisine.

The next morning, we had a light breakfast at the hotel—coffee and home-baked cinnamon buns —and headed back to the airport. I met my new pilot—Amelie, it turned out, a her not a him; a woman at the helm which, I'll admit, though I am no sexist, was a pleasant surprise. I talked to Pablo's pilot and told him to head back to Mérida, thinking I'd call Pablo and catch up with him—not least about my newest acquisition—when we got back to Miami, and Xavier and I settled in for my maiden flight in my very own jet.

Chapter 19

Sunday, October 25, 2009

I am old-school about some things—sunglasses, as I've mentioned, and reading newspapers; I like real paper with ink that stains your fingers as you turn the pages. Pedro, my houseboy, brings me a whole stack of newspapers with my breakfast, which I most frequently take by my pool, dangling my feet in the cool water while I catch up with the latest in the *New York Times*, the *Washington Post*, the *Miami Herald*, and the *Yucatan Times*. When I travel, my news consumption dips off, sometimes to the point that unless there's a major scandal or worldwide political upheaval of the sort you don't even have to read about—the sort that everyone seems to find out about through osmosis—I don't have any idea what's going on outside of my personal whirlwind.

That was why, when we landed back in Miami and I caught a glimpse of CNN playing in a coffee shop as we walked through the terminal toward the parking garage, I ran for the newsstand, picked up a copy of every paper I could find and sat down immediately to leaf through them.

"Holy fuck."

"What is it?" Xavier asked, still in vacation mode.

"Holy fuck," was all I could say, again, as I pulled my cell from my back pocket and dialed Pablo as fast as my shaking fingers would allow. "Holy *fuck*," I said when he picked up.

Pablo sighed. "This is why I think it is such a good idea you are out of town for a few days, you see?"

Pablo had first mentioned, almost a year before, that a crackdown was coming. That, every once in a while, the cartel bosses had to make some gesture—an offering, a sacrifice—that allowed the US DEA to make a splash in the American press about how they were winning what they called "the war on drugs"—a war they'd been waging for going-on twenty years, and squandered nearly fifty million dollars to sustain, and that was no closer to an end than it had been on the day they'd started it. Fighting a "war on drugs" was as simple-minded as fighting a "war on terrorism". One wouldn't find victory fighting either one of those entities with guns and violence, not when the issue was one of supply and demand—demand for the sort of substances, escapist drugs or radical ideologies, that filled the gap when young people weren't supplied with good education, decent jobs, fair wages was never going to be abated by force. I understood this on a cellular level; it was why I'd started the Aj Tz'ib Academy, in order to give the Mayan kids in my own, small corner of the world a shot at the sort of support that might keep them out of my line of work. What better way to honor Taavi?

Usually a crackdown, as I was given to understand the process, involved setting up an easy bust for the DEA agents working on the border. The kingpins would send ten, twenty, maybe even thirty of their soldiers on what seemed a routine business trip, mostly smuggling a good quantity of the operation's lesser-quality wares across the US border, and then tip-off the narcs. The soldiers rarely, if ever, knew what they were walking into; in every case they were sent in only if they were either deemed to be expendable, or they'd done something that the kingpin for whom they worked deemed unforgiveable: stolen from the cartel, or snitched to an authority. In that case setting them up on a bust was a way of saving the cartel ammo; execution by DEA agent.

This crackdown had turned out to be a whole different breed of animal.

It had taken place the night before, in Calexico, a town on the border of the Mexican city Mexicali in Baja California, an area notorious for its violence—the hunting down of illegal immigrants trying to enter the US by crossing the dangerous body of water known as the All American Canal, and the ferocity of the death and destruction associated with its thriving drug trade. The goods were smuggled from Mexicali into the US in one of two ways, via human-foot power through a series of under-engineered, underground tunnels, or dropped in bins by ultralight planes on the

American side of the border. This is Emiliano's territory—the kingpin who'd knocked out Alvaro with his Titanium Gold Desert Eagle .44 on that tense night in Pablo's bunker in Chuburna and who had, I long suspected but could never in a million years have proved, ordered the job on Alvaro finished, had laid him out, head wholly separated from body, in my bed. The tunnels from Calexico to Mexicali are in greater or lesser repair, and fourteen of Emiliano's soldiers died when DEA agents, tipped off about an operation being carried out in one of the least useable tunnels, collapsed it with some well-placed TNT.

None of that was shocking to me. I had braced for something like this since I first made the commitment to launder drug money. I had been told up front that this sort of housecleaning was necessary from time to time, and I was asked if I had the stomach for it, and was given the opportunity to walk away with no hard feelings if I thought I didn't.

You walk away from an income of over four hundred thousand *a day* before you judge.

What was staggering to me was that Emiliano had also been taken out in the raid. Not in the tunnel. In the den of his sprawling hacienda on the outskirts of Mexicali. With a single bullet to the back of the head—execution by a disciplined and experienced assassin.

"Pablo, I'm— I don't even know what to say. I really liked Emiliano. What can I...? Can I do anything?"

Pablo actually laughed. "You can call Tim and tell him to rearrange the pick-up schedule"—the kingpins' cash, lots of crumpled twenties and fifties and hundred-dollar bills, was picked up by armored truck that ran to every corner of the country seven days a week, on a rotating schedule. "No more pick-up anywhere in Baja until I tell you so."

"All right. Sure, Pablo."

"And you'll stay in Miami until I tell you to come back. Use the plane, I don't have a need—"

"Yeah, well, see, I bought a plane today—my own plane. Yours is already on its way back to Mérida."

Pablo laughed again, heartily this time. The laughter, considering what had just happened to Emiliano—someone I'd thought we both *liked* —was disconcerting. "You finally jumped, yes, Clint? At last you trust the money faucet will continue to flow?"

"Yes."

But did I? Was "yes" the correct answer to that last question? Was the housecleaning underway in Mexico a reason to reconsider my sources of future income?

Xavier was standing over me. He was hearing only my side of the conversation, but he was following it better than I was. He handed me a paper cup of bourbon he'd picked up at the nearby airport bar. My hands were still shaking so hard when I picked it up I splashed some on the front of my shirt as I gulped it down.

"Pablo, what about Emiliano!"

Pablo replied with silence. I could almost hear him thinking. "You do not concern yourself with this, Clint. There will be justice for my friend... but you, also my friend, you stay out of my way while I find it for him, yes?"

I wished Xavier had ordered me a double. "Yes, Pablo."

Chapter 20

THE headlines in the newspapers were sensa-
tional. "Fourteen Cartel Members Blown Away
by DEA" (as if taking out a little over a dozen
foot soldiers had put a dent in a trillion-dollar,
intercontinental operation; like crowing about
how, in firing fourteen file clerks, Goldman Sachs
had saved enough of their AIG bailout money to
pay back the government in full. With interest.).
"DEA agents seize over fifty kilograms of cocaine
in violent raid at US Southern border" (as if that
was some sort of remarkable portion of the almost
18,000 kilograms that actually made it into the US
in 2009). "Notorious Mexican kingpin Emiliano
'the Baker' Cassillo, assassinated at home over
weekend, Mexican Navy intelligence credited" (as
if 'the Baker' was a derogatory nickname—the guy
liked bread and he had a way with a baguette—or
Mexican Navy intelligence had a damned thing to
do with his death. Pablo had given me very little
information surrounding Emiliano's assassination, but even I knew, from the manner in which
he'd been hit, that law enforcement had simply
not been involved).

I stood at the island in the Cohen's kitchen and sifted through the half-dozen papers I'd picked up at the airport, marveling over the increasing salaciousness of the coverage of what spokespeople for the US Department of Justice were calling "a major drug bust", and tying it to the murder of Emiliano. But I was an insider; it didn't take much careful reading between the lines at all to figure out that while these two events may have been coordinated, they were in no way related to one another. The raid itself I understood as the cost of doing business; the real mystery was why someone had targeted *Emiliano*.

I thought about turning on the TV set that sat on a shelf over the breakfast nook, maybe find out a few more details from reporters on CNN or MSNBC, but I wasn't really sure how much I was comfortable knowing at just that moment and then, before natural curiosity could win out over fear, Jack wheeled David into the room, moving aside one of the nook's dining chairs to seat him at the breakfast table. Jack had been staying at his parents' house, in his old boyhood room, comforting himself in this time of his father's illness with proximity, and he was wearing an outfit—pleated khaki trousers and a neon orange Ralph Lauren cotton sweater—that had most certainly been pulled from his teenaged closet. The outfit proved Jack had stayed in shape since high school, and that either his taste in fashion or fashion itself had much matured since the early 1990s. David wore a pair of dark-burgundy silk pajamas under a short, chocolate-brown, light cashmere cardigan, and brown leather slippers on his feet. Candace followed them, perfectly turned out, as always, in an elegant morning outfit—beautifully fitted white slacks and a matching shell, her nails blood red, her lips pale pink, and her blonde hair pulled back in a bun that only looked casually tousled.

David's day nurse, Henrietta, a slim, no-nonsense Latina, doled out his morning dose of medications into a small ceramic dish, brought them to him with a glass of ice water, and asked if Mrs. Cohen would like her to prepare the patient's breakfast. Cooking wasn't part of her duties, but Henrietta, to Candace's everlasting gratitude, was one of those people who always went the extra mile and rarely had to be asked to do it.

"Thanks, Henry," Candace replied, "I'll take care of it." Candace pulled a carton of eggs from the refrigerator and a loaf of seeded, gluten-free bread from the freezer, and Henry retreated from the kitchen, understanding that what we all required at the moment was privacy. "Anyone else for a soft-boiled egg?" Candace asked.

Jack and I declined; Candace shrugged and plopped two eggs, one for herself and one for David, in a small pot of cold water and set it to boil.

"Can I at least have a pat of butter on that cardboard bread you want me to eat?" David asked, surprising us all with how his enunciation had improved in just a couple of days. His skin color had improved dramatically too, although his right hand still rested elegantly but uselessly in his lap.

"Absolutely not," Candace told him. "But I'll cut it into soldiers for you to dip, and I'll have a dry slice with my egg too."

"Suffering with me, darling?" David teased her.

"Of course," said Candace. "Let me at least get you boys some coffee." She poured us cups from the pot the housekeeper had already brewed.

David sipped greedily from the half-cup she allowed him before he spoke. "I need you two to take care of an important errand for me today." He put down his cup to pick up the linen napkin Candace had provided and dabbed at his lips; he was still speaking slowly and deliberately, and having a bit of an issue with his mouth, the spittle that collected at the corners because of his lack of muscle control.

"Of course, Dad," Jack said quickly. "Whatever you need, you know that."

David smiled his lopsided grin. "I suppose a more prudent man would have waited to hear what the task was before he agreed to it."

"Well," Jack countered, "I am nothing if not prudent."

David laughed out loud. "I really do need you to pay a visit to Abe."

Jack did an actual double-take. David and Candace hadn't visited their elder son in all the months since he'd taken up residence at the Miami Federal Correctional Institution. Certainly I hadn't darkened the prison doorway either—Abe and I had never been each other's biggest fans. Jack had gone once to visit his brother but come away thoroughly disgusted with his sibling. Abe hadn't asked after the well being of their elderly parents, the whereabouts of his young children, or even the fate of his accomplice in the embezzlement that had put him behind bars, the criminally beautiful Charlotte Cruet who'd stolen both the Cohen's money and my heart; he'd cared only that Jack deliver a message to the ex-wife who had exposed his crime: "Tell her to go fuck herself." After that one visit, Jack had sworn to cut all ties with him.

Just the day before we'd all had a good laugh at the idea of either of us, Jack or me, being a suitable envoy to the Miami Federal Correctional Institution.

"In jail?" Jack asked now, incredulously. "You want me to visit him in jail?"

"That's where he lives," Candace replied, ever reasonable.

Jack's face was slack with disbelief. "*Why*?" he whined.

"Because," David said, "I want all the requirements met, and in short order; we can't afford to dilly-dally any longer about him formally releasing his shares in the bank. Also, I've revised my will, but my cash bequest to him comes with a few strings attached. I need him to understand the terms."

Jack cocked his head, more interested now.

"You"—he pointed at Jack—"will be responsible for administering the trust through which he will receive his cash each month. You will not disperse his monthly stipend if he is *not*, on the day the disbursement is to be made, gainfully employed in a legal industry, if he has *not* at least once in the preceding thirty-day period visited his children for a period of a minimum of thirty-six hours, and if a test proves he is *not* drug-free. In the case of his death, all remaining funds in the trust will become the property of his children, and you will administer their trust until they reach they age of twenty-five or graduate from college, whichever comes first. In the event, Jack, that you predecease your brother"—here David turned to me —"you will take over administration of the trust, Clint."

And there I was, thinking that nothing could have shocked me more than David turning over his bank shares to me in his will. Now *this*. I hadn't realized that David's trust in his elder son had been so broken he would, quite consciously, punish him by putting him under the thumbs of the two people he himself disliked above all others. For the rest of his life.

"I want Abe's signature on a document that attests these terms have been explained to him and that he understands them—and that he will not make any attempt either now or after my death to contest these conditions. Xavier is drawing up a contract that's as ironclad as sheets of paper can be. Make sure you pick it up at his office before you head off to see Abe."

Jack and I looked at each other. Our faces reflected our identical emotional journeys: one part terror at having to confront the man who'd bullied us from the time we were toddlers, even if the confrontation was—blessedly—occurring while he was behind bars and being guarded by men who were armed; and another part undiluted, unmitigated glee that we were being handed such enormous power over our one-time tormentor. For the rest of his life. And he was going to *hate* it.

I was surprised that neither of us lost his cool and laughed out loud.

Chapter 21

Monday, October 26, 2009

A person doesn't just show up at a federal prison, knock on the front door, and ask if Abe Cohen is home and might he come out to play. Jack was still on Abe's visitors' list, though he hadn't used the privilege for months; I sat on the sofa in Jack's office at the bank while his secretary faxed my paperwork to another secretary at the Miami Federal Correctional Institution so that I, too, could be cleared to show up for a chat with Abe on visitor's day.

While we waited, Jack worked at his computer, monitoring the daily transfers into the suspended accounts of the elderly and disabled—money that would be transferred out and into the pseudonymous accounts of my kingpins within seconds after it hit the original recipient's account—no error, no foul, and no trace on the account holder's statement of any activity.

I'd already spoken at length that morning with Miguel, and gone over the plans I'd sketched out for the library improvements on my last night in

Mérida; the conversation I'd had with Tim Gustav, my assistant in Mexico who was monitoring the transfers from the other end, was just as banal. My school was both architecturally satisfying and filled with thriving students, and the drug money was flowing easily; and the thought crossed my mind—as it had been crossing my mind ever since the laundry business had started operating so efficiently that it had become mundane—*damn, but I could use a little excitement.* It helped to remember that a visit to Abe was in my near future, and that would surely prove to be an invigorating experience. Thinking about duking it out with witless Abe—even though the battle would, of necessity, be confined to words—took the edge off.

"The Feds might give me a pass"—I shivered with adrenaline at the thought that Jack's secretary was in the process of faxing approval for them to run a background check on me, though I knew they'd find nothing incriminating; I was just any other wealthy businessman, on paper— "but doesn't Abe have some say over who gets in to see him? I mean, I know they're not running a concierge service over there, but does he have to show up in the visitors' room at the whim of just anyone who files the right forms with the state?"

Jack took a drag of his cigarette before he answered. It wasn't entirely legal, his lighting up in his own office; his own HR team enforced workplace safety regulations and would have frowned at his actions, if they'd known about them. His secretary, however, was a secret smoker as well and, for the privilege of being able to escape into the boss's office once or twice a day for a quick smoke break, she happily doused his carpet and curtains with Febreze several times a day—and always before a scheduled meeting with a board member—and emptied the ashtray he kept in his top desk drawer before she left to go home at night. Then she smuggled the dead butts out of the building like contraband. Nobody but Jack and his secretary thought they were getting away with a damned thing.

"The prisoners have to request any addition to their visitor list." Jack laughed, "I like to think Abe pissed his pants when his C.O. told him Avril called to say you wanted in to see him. Anyway, he would absolutely not turn you away if you just showed up in the visitors' room, Clint, any more than he'd turn me away. He's just a big, mean, dumbass and his curiosity about what we want with him overpowers any urge he might have to try to be cool."

Jack's secretary, the secret smoker Avril, poked her head into his office. "Hey, so, all the paper-work has been faxed over. When I did this for your clearance, Jack, it took them two days to respond." Avril slid through the door and leaned against it, fishing a lighter and a pack of Benson & Hedges out of her pocket. She gestured at me with her unlit cigarette. "If you're sitting in here waiting for a reply, you might want to think about coming back on Wednesday."

I looked at Jack, who shrugged. "I know how we can kill some time."

It promised, at the outset, to be a day of real estate porn. Our first stop was an abandoned bank building in South Miami that Jack had recently acquired. Citizens National had no office yet in that particular exurb and Jack always had his feelers out for expansion: the more small branch offices we had to process the drug money, the faster and more securely our daily transfer amounts could grow. Eight million a day was a dent in the bucket in terms of the fortunes these Mexican businessmen owned; the more I could accelerate the in-take rate, the more our profits could swell.

"It's in the older part of town," Jack had informed me, and that designation conjured certain scenery, an historic district, now-dilapidated but waiting for a loving hand, a big dream, and an even bigger pocketbook. I visualized a promising Art Deco gem from the area's golden era, or some space-aged Atomic Architecture prize—either way something ripe for renovation.

I was so disappointed when Jack pulled up in front of our bank's newest branch I would have sworn my blood pressure dropped. Our new building was the fugliest, falling-down, pre-fab shithole I'd ever seen—a relic of the Urban Renewal Era, a faux-stone and turquoise aluminum facaded monstrosity that had, in all likelihood, been built in the late 1960s to replace what had been an Art Deco gem. Sadly, I could see the early years of the 20th Century reflected in almost every other building on the street. Jack bumped into one of the six, narrow, pot-holed parking spaces directly in front of the old bank. When he unlocked the padlock on the chain that was wound through the handles on the double front glass doors, we heard a crash from the back of the building—bottles toppling; glass shattering.

"Mice?" I asked.

"Poachers?" Jack wondered.

"Someone taking out his recycling?"

"Should I call the police?"

I sighed and looked around. There was nothing about the dark, dank building that invited exploration. At least not the sort of excursion that was worth risking one's life for. What if it was poachers back there in the dark? I could almost see the germs and bacteria writhing on the once-green indoor/outdoor carpeting; I could smell the mold in the walls. I pointed overhead, to a gaping hole that had been, at one time, a skylight. "I think our best bet is going to be to just tear this fucker down and rebuild from the ground up."

"Really?" I heard the hopeful note in his voice; I was the resident expert in construction and he wanted to believe my diagnosis.

"Really, Jack. Let's get the hell out of here and call the demo crew."

The next three stops on our real estate tour were located in the same cul de sac: the three bungalows Eddie had been in the middle of flipping when he'd been hit by the dune buggy. They were all in the same neighborhood in the Grove, all bought as foreclosures, all small, two-bedroom places, stripped down to bare boards, their 1970s-era small, separate kitchen, dining, and living rooms being opened up to accommodate the open-plans most current home buyers valued.

"He had the right instincts," I said to Jack, inspecting the floor plans Eddie had sketched out and the drywall installation that was taking place in the first of the houses we visited. "He also hired workmen who know what they're doing. Depending on the finishes he's chosen—the floor, countertops, and kitchen cabinets—I wouldn't be ashamed to sell this house to a young family at the end of this renovation."

"So," Jack asked, "you're going to let the work continue?"

I looked around at the workman nailing up drywall, the workman installing the new kitchen plumbing, the workman breaking up the old concrete sidewalk outside the front door, and the workman hauling away the shattered chunks of it in a wheelbarrow. "The convenient thing to do is to sell these places as-is. But the estate would take a loss—and how can I, in good conscience, put all of these people out of work? These are their *jobs*, you know. This is how they're feeding their families."

Jack can't always be counted on to back me up. What I mean is, we have been best friends since boyhood and, every once in a while, the twelve-year-olds inside of us will not rest until we have absolutely roasted each other. In this instance, however, Jack would be the first to tell you I'd already made my plea for the workers' jobs, and he'd already offered me his first smarmy comeback—

"Same fucking socialist pussy you've always been, Clint"—before either of us noticed that the workman who was hauling away the concrete wasn't a man. It was most assuredly a woman. A woman with a specific shade of shiny, dark brown hair hanging down her back in a braid, a braid that stretched out of the back of a hardhat, down between two sharp shoulder blades, to a small, plump ass encased in a pair of denim overalls like the dot at the end of an exclamation point.

"Jesus Christ, Jack." I was nearly whispering, which you think would have clued him into my state of mind. That he ought not to shout, "What?" back at me so loudly that every head on the site turned to the two of us.

Including Charlotte's.

And she and I, we caught each other's eye.

I was frozen, but Charlotte chucked the chunk of concrete she had just picked up into the pile in the wheelbarrow and started to remove her yellow suede work gloves as she sauntered over toward us.

"How you been, Clint?" she asked, tucking the gloves under one arm and extending the other hand to me.

I had wanted Charlotte to come to Mexico to live with me. I had wanted Charlotte to use the teaching degree she had almost completed when we met in service to my then-unnamed school for the Mayan kids. I had wanted Charlotte to make a life with me.

I had wanted Charlotte.

If human sexual preference were a spectrum, with people who preferred only women at one extreme and people who preferred only men at the other, then I imagined I sat somewhere to the left of dead center, toward the end favoring men but nowhere near the outermost reaches.

I had wanted Charlotte as much as I had ever wanted any woman.

But she had been Abe's accomplice in his embezzlement scheme.

She had tried to rip me off for two million dollars.

I'd caught her and made her turn herself in, give evidence of Abe's crimes so that she would be spared a jail sentence. I was the reason she was free. Free to be out here on this construction site, hauling concrete.

"I've been all right, Charlotte. You?"

She laughed.

"I mean," I stammered, "is this where you're working while you finish your student teaching?"

She laughed even harder. "I'm a felon now, Clint, remember? There's no school district in the country that's going to hire me and put me in a classroom with a bunch of impressionable kids."

I think I was too stunned to nod. All these months since she and Abe were busted and I'd never even thought that the confession I'd required of her would derail her real dream. Only how it would affect Abe. I'd wanted to derail Abe *that* badly.

"You know," Charlotte continued, "there's something I've wanted to tell you. I didn't do any of that shit because I loved Abe and wanted to run away with him. I never thought about even running—not, I mean, except at the very end. When it seemed like a good solution. For about a split second. I wasn't even going to get a lot of money out of it. Abe was supposed to be the big beneficiary. I was going to get a cut that would have been enough to pay off my student loans, and the mortgage on my dad's house. I'm not like you, Clint. I don't have big dreams. I never did, not even before the only job I could get was as part of a demolition crew."

I think, if Charlotte had had a chunk of the concrete in her hands, she would have flung it at my feet.

And maybe I would have deserved it.

When Jack dropped me off at my condo, I invited him up for a beer. I didn't want to be alone, but he had plans—a date he'd made before his dad had had a stroke, and I'd been banished to Miami, and Eddie had died. He wanted to keep it—"The dude's so hot, Clint," he promised. He'd stayed for only one bottle before taking off.

I popped a second when I'd shut the door behind him. I wondered how long it was going to be until Pablo gave me the OK to return to Mexico. I wondered what was going on *in* Mexico, but none of the newspapers I'd asked the building's concierge to send up offered any more detail about the drug bust than I already knew.

I went to the sink in the kitchen to wash the newsprint off my hands, feeling like a visitor in my own country, the very city in which I'd grown up and lived most of my still-short life. Miami was no longer my real home.

I realized, however, that, while Miami could be a fucking circus, it wasn't hell, and I had responsibilities here now to attend to. Doing my part in David's on-going care; even if that meant only visiting him frequently and doing something to lighten Candace's load. Eddie's memorial service to attend. His estate to settle. His flips to supervise. A bank branch to build. Jack to hang out with. Jack's brother to visit in jail.

And, even so, I wondered what I was going to do with my time until Pablo called me home. I slouched against the sink and thought about Laine Gordon—about maybe calling her and inviting her out to dinner. We'd shared Eddie's death; it seemed right to show my appreciation for how well she'd taken care of him by taking her out for a steak and a bottle of wine. See if she was still as cute as I remembered from that terrible night we'd had together. And up for splashing around a little in the dating pool.

I reached behind me to toss my empty in the sink, and leaned forward to reach into the refrigerator for a third Sol when a thought occurred to me so suddenly that I stood up with a startle. I had to go visit Elmer Collier. I had to go to the nursing home to visit Eddie's grandfather, a man I hadn't seen in person since I was a kid and he'd been swinging a bucket and a mop down the hall of my prep school. It was my responsibility now to be his representative with the nursing home staff, and how was I possibly going to accomplish that without actually going to the goddamned nursing home?

"Oh, fuck me," I muttered, and downed the third Sol in six long, bracing gulps.

Chapter 22

I did call Laine for a date. That afternoon I took her to Sunshire, the nursing home where Eddie moved his grandfather when his fortunes had improved. It was a pretext, of sorts—a lame one; claiming to want a doctor's opinion concerning the quality of care my new legal dependent was receiving—but she agreed.

Let me go on the record: a nursing home is not a good first-date option.

Sunshire itself is gorgeous, a former hospital—one built sometime in the 1940s, with the character that public buildings had in the days before we stopped caring about how our public spaces look. On the outside, four, two-story, aggressively spray-washed granite columns hold up the front portico of a pristine red brick edifice, its white trim freshly painted. Inside, once-antiseptic hospital halls have been transformed into wide-open spaces done in an American traditional style—dark wood wainscoting, a fireplace at nearly every turn, plush carpeting, and cushy upholstery on wide sofas and tall wingchairs. I had braced myself for the smell—that peculiar, hospital-y aroma, a perfume with a top note of disinfectant and a base note of urine. But inside Sunshire I could smell... nothing. Oh, I got a whiff of something Chanel when a distinguished-looking woman, her thick gray hair in a perfect French twist, passed by me, slowly, with her walker, and I caught the scent coming from the dining room, something roast-beefy that made me realize I was hungry. But, other than that—nothing. The cool air was stunningly neutral, and clean.

The staff consisted mostly of young people, around my own age, I suspected. All of them were dressed casually, in no particularly uniform way—sweat pants or tights or jeans, tee-shirts or tunics, less as if they were paid caretakers than superbly helpful grandchildren who'd just dropped by for a visit. Each of them had a smile on his or her face that seemed genuine.

"May I help you?" a bright-eyed Hispanic woman stationed at the reception desk asked as Laine and I pushed through the front doors.

"Yes, Clint Kennedy"—I held out one hand for her to shake and used the other to point to my companion—"Laine Gordon. Dr. Laine Gordon."

"Mr. Kennedy. Dr. Gordon."

"I'm Mr. Elmer Collier's new legal guardian—I'm sure my attorney has already faxed you the paperwork. I wanted to stop by to get a look at the facility. To make sure Mr. Collier's in good hands."

I might as well have said "Abracadabra." The oldest employee I'd seen yet—a woman maybe in her mid-forties, so that isn't saying much—hustled out of the office that was glassed-off behind the reception area. Her attire was more standard business than the rest of the employees, and she moved quickly and purposefully on respectably high heels.

"Donna McAdam"—she held out her hand to Laine, then to me—"I'm the Managing Director of Sunshire Elder Care Home, the original facility built by the Sunshire Retirement Corporation, and the architectural and spiritual model for all of SRC's elder-care facilities. Let me show you around!"

Donna was a whirlwind, keeping up a steady stream of descriptive chatter as she led us from small TV and reading rooms, to a large recreation room that boasted both shuffleboard and ping-pong, to a gleaming gym/PT wing, to the well-stocked library, to the on-premises beauty salon and barbershop, to the arts and craft room, to the massage room, to the steam room, to a music room stocked with several guitars (one electric), a shelf of various brass instruments in their cases, plus a violin, and a gleaming black Steinway piano by the fireplace. I allowed myself a *plunk* on the keys as we passed by and was pleased to note that it was in tune as well. Every place we looked appeared to have been dusted or vacuumed only moments before, and every resident we saw was either engaged in some apparently satisfying group activity or a one-on-one with someone of the young staff. The patient-to-staff ratio at Sunshire seemed to me, on casual count, to be about two-to-one. All the while we toured, Donna kept up a running commentary about the perks of the place, everything from the fact that the cut flowers on the coffee- and side- and dining tables were replaced with fresh ones twice a week, and, at Sunshire, doctors were not merely on-call but on-premises twenty-four/seven.

With the assurance that a doctor was never farther than an elevator ride away at Sunshire at any given time of the day, she ushered us into one of a bank of four elevators off the reception area and whisked us up to the floors that contained the patients' rooms, and to our patient, Mr. Elmer Collier.

On Elmer's floor, while the rooms were just as beautifully appointed as they were on every other floor—freshly painted, furnished traditionally, and with good-quality pieces—the beds weren't dark wood four-posters but standard hospital fare. Nurses, hidden among the sweats-attired personnel on the lower floors, stood out here in colorful scrubs. The smell was less pleasant, but the patient-to-staff ratio on this floor seemed to be reversed, one-to-two.

Donna stood aside at one of the doors just past a nurse's station. "Mr. Collier," she said, waving us into his room with the sweep of an arm and a finger to her lips. "He's sleeping right now. I'll give you a moment, but I'll be right outside," she whispered as she slipped through the door and closed it behind her.

I hung back. Laine went right up to the bed where Elmer lay. I hated myself for this, but the first thought that went through my mind was, well, any hope I had that this date was going to go well is over now. It was more pleasant than my second thought which was, well, *get a good look because that's going to be you someday on a bed like that.*

Laine, however, focused first on the patient. I watched as she examined him, gently touching his face, his palm, his foot, assessing the equipment arrayed around him and what it could tell her about his condition. I saw her grin as she saw that in this loveliest of institutional rooms, there were framed family photos on Elmer's bedside table, and an upturned book, as if someone had been reading to him.

She came, at last, to stand beside me again. "I'm most impressed," she said, "that he's clearly getting a good, thorough bath every day." She looked up at me, smiled and proclaimed, "Elmer Collier is in very good hands at Sunshine."

I smiled back at her. "That's good to know."

The time with Elmer, brief as it was, had put me in a somber mood, so Donna's good will when we exited his room felt sudden and overwhelming. "Right this way, now, Dr. Gordon, Mr. Kennedy," she said, leading us along the corridor, back to the elevators. "The one thing I haven't shown you yet is our dining room, and you must be my guests for lunch—"

"Oh," I interrupted, "that's not—"

"Nonsense," Donna cut me off. "You have to have lunch with us. Our executive chef comes directly to us with four-stars!"

"Four stars? Four *Michelin* stars? Not buying it," I said when Laine and I were seated at one of the two dozen, cloth-draped, flower-adorned tables, ours one of the tables-for-two, discreetly to one side.

"No, really." Laine showed me the screen of the iPhone she'd been furiously tapping at. "He came from Shikany."

"One of my favorites and, still, not even one-star."

"Oh, let's just taste the food, and let that speak for itself." She picked up the menu card at her place. "You have the pot roast, I'll have the lemon chicken, and we can compare notes."

A waitress—dressed in typical waiter gear of black pants, white buttoned-down shirt, and a long white apron—took our order and poured more water into our tumblers before leaving us alone.

"This is not what I had in mind, Laine, when I asked you to go to lunch."

Laine smiled. She had a great smile— Hell, she had a great face, one of the greatest faces of all time, in my book—and any chemistry between us had either existed only in my fevered imagination on the night we spent together in the hospital, or been thoroughly doused during our nursing-home tour.

I started laughing so hard I had to put my head in my hands to get myself back in control. When I looked up, I saw that Laine had been laughing too.

"So why *did* you ask me to come here with you?"

"I don't know. I wanted your opinion about Sunshire. I wanted to ask you out." I shrugged. "I like you."

Laine reached across the table and touched my hand. "I like you too.," And then she withdrew her hand and continued, "I like how much you care."

I nodded. "I'm firmly in the friend zone, aren't I?" I asked her.

She giggled and nodded. "I think that's right where you want to be."

"Why would you say that?"

She threw her head back and laughed as fully as I had. "Because who does this?" she hiss-whispered at me, gesturing around at our surroundings.

I scrambled for an answer, but the question was clearly rhetorical.

"I'll tell you who…" Laine smiled. "…a lonely guy who wants a little company, a little conversation, a little sexual tension—but, deep inside, the guy across the table from me? He's really wishing I were someone else…"

I would have interrupted her, but the thought of Taavi raced too quickly to my mind for me to form words. My face felt hot. I was sure it was an awful shade of pink.

And then I thought of Charlotte and wondered if I might spontaneously implode.

"See?" Laine asked, stirring a slice of lemon in her tumbler of water with her straw. "See what I'm talking about?"

Chapter 23

Tuesday, October 27, 2009

"THE unexamined life is not worth living." It has become conventional wisdom to accept the truth of this dictum, but, for me, this is another famous moral tidbit with which I take issue. I think the whole concept of an examined life has been oversold. I mean, not that solitude and re-flection are innately bad things—we all need a day every once in a while with our feet in the shallow end of a blue pool and a cold beer in our hand —but, truly, sustained navel-gazing is acceptable for only two groups of people: the very young who have yet to figure out what, for them, makes life worth living; and the very old who are, some with delight and others with bitterness, looking back on lives already lived and taking the measure of their worth. You spend too much time in between your eighteenth birthday and your eightieth try-ing to examine every goddamned thing you do, then there is no time for the actual *doing*. Too many productive hours spent in second-guessing, assessing risk, nurturing fear, lead to becoming so cripplingly scared that turning outward, re-turning to the reality that had to be thought over, squarely facing the world and its challenges, be-comes too frightening.

At its most extreme, chronic introspection is how we end up with hermits and actuaries.

The evidence of the worth of an examined life has been, in my opinion, severely skewed, prof-fered at every turn by people who get caught up in the antique sentiment and conveniently forget the context in which Socrates offered it: his trial for corruption. His conviction to the words he uttered in that circumstance, so glaringly incomplete and ill-considered, is what earned him a death sen-tence.

It was with some embarrassment, then, that I sat in the passenger seat of Jack's Porsche, turned from him, my forehead thrumming against the window glass as he sped down Krome Avenue, turning my recent encounter with Charlotte—my whole fucking history with Charlotte—over and over again in my mind. Thoughts of her came to me as GIFs: Charlotte smiling at me as we walked down a wide, white, Mérida boulevard on a sultry Mexican evening, the setting sun tinting the aura around her slicked back hair, her sleek black ponytail, a rosy gold. Charlotte gasping, her mouth forming a pink 'o' of surprise, her pale hand rising to cover her shocked lips as I con-fronted her about her part in Abe's embezzlement scheme. Charlotte in a long braid and overalls, doing her worst on the demolition crew at Eddie's flip.

You are not responsible for her downfall, I reminded myself. *You are not the one who schemed
to steal a couple million bucks. It is entirely her own
fault that she's chucking concrete around in a pair
of muddy and really unattractive steel-toed boots.*

Jack had popped in a new CD he'd just picked
up that morning—he was in a country phase and
it was all Reba, all *ain't love strange*, all the time
as we drove. *Oh, fuck*, I muttered to myself while
Reba wailed. *Ain't love strange.* My consolation
was that Jack's own bleating attempt at car pool
karaoke drowned out anything he might have
heard me mumble.

Good date last night? I thought to ask him this,
but I was pretty confident he thought I was just
asleep, my head banging off the window in some
sweet dream, and I decided to leave well enough
alone.

Manuel Noriega, Lou Pearlman, Anthony "Marsh-
mallow" Mannarino—these were among the names
Abe dropped after Jack and I had been X-rayed
and patted down and, generally, made it through
the hoops the Miami Federal Correctional Institution set up for us and wormed our way inside its
gates. Abe was escorted into a small, windowless
room to meet us, ambling up to the table where
Jack and I sat in hard-backed chairs, just as if he
were an eighth grader about to give two twelve-
year-olds the business during lunch period.

"What do you two losers want?" he asked. It
was a question, I realized, that was only partially
a joke; Abe, in his inadequate but still-beating

heart of hearts, really did think Jack and I were the schlemiels with a problem.

I decided to take the high road. "Hey, Abe, lookin' good," I told him, because he really had lost a lot of weight. I hadn't seen him look so healthy since before he'd hit puberty and the hormones had played havoc with his metabolism—and this in spite of the loose skin that wobbled at his jawline and gathered at his dimpled elbows and sat like a pudding at his waist.

He grunted in reply and dropped that string of illustrious names, ticking off all the high-class criminals who'd become his acquaintances in the pen.

"Wow," Jack beamed at his brother, "ya think ya can get us some autographs?"

"Fuck off, you little cocksucker," Abe growled as he took the third chair at the table.

"Speaking of"—Jack's already overblown grin brightened, "how *is* prison sex? It seems so hot in all the pornos..."

I stifled a hot laugh as Abe startled, his now-skinny ass hovering over the seat of his chair. I wondered if Jack had gone too far and Abe was going to call for the guard to end this interview. I was rather relieved when Abe wiggled his bony butt and plopped it in the chair. In spite of the fact that this scenario—Abe in jail and at our mercy—was like a pre-teen ultimate fantasy come to life, Jack and I were here for David. Much as I might delight in taunting Abe, we had business to conduct; I reached under the table and smacked Jack's knee:

stop trying to piss off your brother and get on with it.

Jack had carried in the manila envelope that was stuffed with the paperwork Xavier had prepared. It sat before him on the table; he reached now and pushed it toward Abe. "Dad had a stroke a couple of days ago," he said and paused, waiting for Abe to express concern for their father's health. Abe remained silent and I could almost see the molten steel being poured as if into the center of Jack's vertebral column. "He's going to be fine, you selfish bastard, but it made him realize he had to get a few things in order. Like his will. Which he's changed." Jack used the forefinger and thumb of his right hand like a spring, to flick the manila envelope closer to Abe. "Read it, fuck face."

Jack and I sat quietly, looking at neither Abe nor each other while Abe read. A uniformed guard waited just on the other side of the room's heavy metal door. I watched him through the door's wired window, marveling at the professionalism of his display of disinterest, wondering at the kind of interior life—*introspection, examination*—one would necessarily have to create for one's self if one's job was to wait on felons while they spoke to their lawyers and other loved ones, all the time both appearing discreet and remaining vigilant for violence. What *was* that man thinking? *I need to pick up milk on the way home*, or *Go ahead, do something funny, inmate, I'm looking to draw a little blood today*. Did he have to work very hard at maintaining such a thoroughly unremarkable appearance? I squinted my eyes and tried to think of one thing I would say to describe the man—one thing beyond 'about six feet tall, two-twenty or so, fat nose with several blackheads that needed attention, no facial hair. Or head hair. White.'

Abe's cackle interrupted my reverie. "Is he fucking loony? Did that stroke totally take out Dad's —" He tapped his forehead.

"Brain, Abe?" I offered.

"There's no fucking way I'm signing any of this, agreeing to you two being my babysitters for the rest of my life. He's a goddamn loony loon if he thinks that's going to fly with me—" Abe paced the small room, seeming to break out into a sweat as we watched.

"That fucking cheap bastard and his cunt wife are trying to cut me out of my own inheritance? If I'm lucky, those lousy traitors will die before they can carry out their sick plan."

"Abe,"—Jack stopped him—"don't you see? You no longer have a choice about these things. Notice"—Jack gestured at the plain room around us, the wired window, the inscrutable guard on the other side of it—"where you are, brother."

Abe grinned. "I know exactly where I am, *brother*," he said. "More important, I know exactly who I am, and who you are, the two of you, you sniveling little fags—"

"Bi," I interjected.

Abe's brow furrowed. "What?"

"Bi," Jack repeated. "Clint's bi. Accuracy on this point means a lot to him."

"You rotten fucking cocksuckers," Abe bellowed loudly enough that the inscrutable, stoic guard took note. "Take your stinking pieces of paper"— the pages, followed by the manila envelope, fluttered through the air around our heads—"and get the hell out of here. And what you think about when you get on the other side of the barbed wire is this: you think about what you're going to need to do to get Dad to remove these contingencies from my inheritance. You think real hard and long about that because I don't know what scheme you've got going down in Mexico, but I know it can't be legal. Legal businesses don't make the kind of money I saw you guys sucking in there at the end. Nothing legal could have saved the bank until you stepped in, Clint. The only thing to do was exactly what I was doing—get the cream off the top and get out of town. But, all of a sudden, there's Clint... and we've got a faucet with millions of bucks just gushing out and right into our vault." Abe cackled again, a noise somewhere between a grunt and a belly laugh. "Fuck, I don't know what kind of scam you two are running, but I know it's a doozy, and if my rightful share of it comes with strings, with you two fuckers hanging over my head... Well, I don't see why I'd let you get away with your share of it either."

Both Jack and I sat back in our chairs, processing Abe's words.

"You'd blow up the family business just to try to prove your asinine point?" Jack wondered.

Abe grinned. "In a fucking heartbeat."

Jack and I stood on the other side of the barbed wire. I was sucking in the fresh air and Jack was fumbling with his lighter and a fresh pack of cigarettes.

"Well," I gasped, "that went well."

Chapter 24

"IF I tell Pablo about what Abe said—" There was no way to be gentle about this. "Jack, if I tell Pablo that Abe has threatened the laundry work ... Abe is dead. That's it. Abe's a dead man."

"You know, I don't really give a shit. I really don't—"

"No, no, you really do—"

"Why should I?"

I had to think. "Your mother. Candace would not be happy if Abe were dead."

"She's the only one."

The conversation was more rapid-fire than it might seem from the words on this page, conducted around the punching bag in the gym at Jack's condo, nearly every phrase punctuated with Jack landing a solid smack.

We'd headed to Jack's as soon as we'd returned from the prison and took turns in his gray-and-copper slate shower with its dozen different rain-forest-style heads, steaming the aura of jailhouse off ourselves. Then we threw on shorts and tee-shirts and headed to the gym. The building's gym facility was on the small side, but it was gleaming clean and cleverly fitted with a wide range of equipment. Jack and I had entered with the intentions of putting in a few miles on a couple of the treadmills that stood in a line against the back wall—maybe catching up on our news consumption, watching a couple of cable news broadcasts on the TV that was braced above the running machines while we were at it. But, then, we entered the actual room. We saw the new piece of equipment standing in the center of it. A four-foot tall, sturdy cylinder swathed in black vinyl, hanging by silver chains from the ceiling. A brand new 100-pound training bag.

It being the middle of the day, there was no one else in the gym that saw its busiest hours between five and seven AM and again between six and eight PM, all the corporate types who clustered in this condo development getting in their pre- or post-work workouts. No one around but the trainer, who sat behind a reception desk filling in a staffing grid. As no one else was around, we felt emboldened to let the trainer lace us up in gloves and give us a few training-bag pointers.

And then we laced into that training bag as if it were every enemy either of us had ever accumulated—Abe, and Alvaro, and even that stroke itself that had sidelined David. I'd hold the bag while Jack punched the fucking stuffing out of it, and then we'd switch up and he'd hold it for me.

"I mean"—I said, drawing back for my attack—"on the other hand, I have to tell him. I have to tell Pablo. If I don't, it would be grounds for..."

I landed a punch that would have taken the bag out had it been a living being. "If I *don't* tell him, and he finds out—which he *will* find out—then I become the person who lied to him."

"Don't lie to him. Just don't tell him."

"A lie of omission. My kingpins are Catholics, Jack, they know the rules."

"Right."

"But"—I completed a series of roundhouse kicks that left both myself and Jack panting from the exertion—"if I come clean, then I'm still the honest broker, and I have influence over how Pablo deals with the situation."

"That makes sense."

"What doesn't make sense," I gasped, leaning against the Nautilus Bowflex while I caught my breath, "is that Abe would both have the idea that we're into something illegal, and still be so fearless in challenging it. I mean, he has to know that, if we aren't all on the up-and-up, then you and I surely aren't the muscle of the outfit. Is he too stupid to entertain the thought that, if we are as he believes we are, we have to have partners, and they have to be a whole lot more dangerous than the two of us?"

Jack walked to the water cooler while he thought. "Yes. He's that stupid." He handed me a cup of cold water. "He is that fucking stupid and then some."

"Ah."

He guzzled his water, then crushed the paper cup into a ball and aimed it at the waste can by the cooler, banking his shot. "Here's another thought."

"Yes?"

"Why do we really need Abe to sign those papers? You know, sure, it would be easier if he did, but there's nothing that will keep Dad from writing his own will as he chooses, whether Abe cooperates or not. We just forget we even tried, let Abe go back to his prison life as if we'd never made the trip—"

"And hope Abe forgets our request as well?"

"Exactly."

"And lie to your dad? Just let him think we did as he asked? Think we could pull that off?"

Jack grunted. "We might slip under Dad's radar —at least until he's feeling better. But Mom? She'd sniff us out in a New York minute." Jack reached into the pocket of his workout shorts and withdrew his cell. "I do have this as backup," he said and hit a couple of buttons until I heard Abe's voice: "That fucking cheap bastard and his cunt wife are trying to cut me out of my own inheritance? If I'm lucky, those lousy traitors will die before they can carry out their sick plan."

I took off my shirt and used it to wipe the sweat that was running down my face. "That won't sway Pablo, you know. Only your parents. How did you even get your phone inside the jail? And why would you even want to? To record that? You know you can never let your mom and dad hear it."

Jack shrugged and thumbed the cell again, to turn off Abe's abhorrent voice. "I know."

"So that still leaves us explaining to Pablo, as precisely and with as much humility as possible, what Abe is threatening—and we make sure he understands that the best way to shut him up doesn't involve actually just killing the fucker."

Jack threw a leg over an ab board and leaned back against it. "I don't really want him dead, you know."

"I know. That's why we're going to arrange it so that's not how he ends up."

"Clint."

"Ah, yes. Hi, Pablo." Jack and I had left the gym and gone back to his condo where I'd taken yet another shower—this one to cleanse my head as well as my body—and downed a bottle of Sol and a shot of Patron Silver—for the courage—and dialed Pablo's cell. He'd answered too quickly, on the first ring, as if he'd been waiting for my call. "How are you, Pablo?" I stammered, a stupid question to someone I knew full well had neither the time nor the inclination for small talk these days.

"You are calling about Matamoros."

"Ah, yes. Matamoros..." I hadn't a fucking clue what he was talking about, but as I repeated the name of the town, I clipped Jack on the back of his head—"Right, *Matamoros*..."—and he dutifully jumped onto his laptop to try to find out the significance of the Mexican border town while I vamped. "Not that I'm trying to pry or anything, of course, I just heard, you know, and I thought I ought to give you a call and..."

Jack pushed his MacBook Pro across his coffee table so I could see what he'd found—scan the article in the Brownsville, Texas *Herald* that described the pre-dawn DEA raid on the little town just across its border, a town so close to Brownsville that stray bullets from the shoot-out in Matamoros that had taken out the twenty-two so-far-confirmed drug smugglers had damaged some of the facades at the University of Texas at Brownsville.

I gulped. "Felipe?"

Matamoros was Felipe's territory, as Mexicali had once been Emiliano's.

"I am sorry to say my friend Felipe is no longer with us."

Felipe, who had been so moved by my school, and the work I was doing to help the Mayan kids, he'd offered himself as a patron.

"Pablo…" I hesitated to ask my next question. Soldiers stupid enough to be either expendable or traitorous, or both, were sacrificed in the raids the kingpins scheduled for the DEA's benefit. Never the kingpins themselves. Pablo was surely as unnerved as I was that two of the nation's top industry moguls had been taken out in so many days. I poured myself another shot of Patron and asked it anyway. "How is it possible that Felipe was in the way of the guns? Where was his protection?"

There were several seconds of silence before Pablo replied. "Felipe was not in the way of the guns. He was in Guerrero, on a fishing trip with some friends. Unfortunately, this afternoon, he was unable to return to shore with his boat."

The seconds were mine now to fill with stunned silence.

"Well, that's just... That's quite a coincidence... That's really, Pablo, so..."

"Unfortunate," Pablo repeated.

"Exactly," I agreed, too heartily.

Jack sat across from me on the sofa, his hands outstretched, upturned, holding his breath waiting to be filled in. His eyes were wide and stricken and I had to turn away from him in order to continue to form responses to Pablo.

"So, then, Pablo, I guess this means no pickups in Tamaulipas until further notice—"

"Oh, no, Clint, my friend, you will pick up the Matamoros money in Nuevo Laredo. Andres will be taking over Felipe's territory and you must have Tim make arrangements with him."

"Of course. I'll... I'll call Tim right away—"

"Please. A truck is due for Andres tomorrow afternoon and we want our transfers to flow smoothly, even with this new wrinkle in the schedule, yes?"

"Yes."

"Good man! You will telephone me tomorrow then, when it is all done, to tell me so."

"I will."

"Good night, then. Until tomorrow," he said, and disconnected.

I sat on Jack's sofa, staring at my phone. It was a way to ignore Jack's slack jaw and shaking hands, begging me for information. "What the fuck, Clint!" he blurted when he could stand it no more.

I shook my head, as if that might shake some words out of my mouth.

"Clint!"

"I don't know, OK?" I splashed another two fingers of Patron into my glass. "I couldn't begin to tell you what's going on in Mexico, only some kind of housecleaning, and I'm grateful as hell Pablo doesn't want me down there right now and mixed up in it."

Chapter 25

JUDGE Errol T. Kushner dipped his fingers into the can of Copenhagen—original Copenhagen; none of that flavored shit for the judge—that sat on top of a stack of custom social stationary in the partially opened right hand drawer of his desk. A slight twist in his black leather, ergonomically-designed reclining office chair and he was positioned directly over the brass spittoon on the floor. For years Kushner had stopped every morning for a cup of coffee, which liquid he dumped out the driver's side door as promptly as he pulled away from the drive-through at the neighborhood Starbucks; the cup was what he wanted. He'd use the cup throughout his day at the office, and then take it with him when he left at night—to use to spit in in the car—and then he'd dump the cup and all of its accumulated, foamy brown, viscous contents in the family trash bin when he pulled into his house in the exclusive Gables Estates. Kushner had earned himself a reputation over the years as a hard-working public servant, getting to the courthouse early in the day and staying sometimes very late into the night when, really, anyone else not as disciplined as the revered jurist would rather be on the tennis court or in the pool or lounging on a porch overlooking the expensive green lawn at his lovely Mediterranean-style mansion.

The truth was, Kushner liked his work. And he was disciplined. One did not rise from the smoky streets of what was arguably the most squalid neighborhood in the most squalid 1970s-era Newark, New Jersey, to graduate, with honors, from Harvard Law without a steely sense of self-control. Nevertheless, his work ethic was one of the virtues for which he was, if not loved, then much respected, though it should be made clear that there were other traits for which he was loved.

Judge Kushner liked his work, and he basked in the office where he did the work. It was a pleasure to drive into an office every day when the office was located in an Art Deco jewel of a courthouse— erected in 1925. There were any number of atrocities that had been committed upon the white limestone courthouse over the decades since it was built—the dropped ceilings, done in the 1970s in order to cut air conditioning costs, being one of the most perverse, in the judge's opinion—but the elegantly etched brass elevator doors remained. The frieze molding and the black-marble water fountain in the lobby remained. The polished walnut paneling still made his office feel like a cool, dark cocoon on even the brightest Florida afternoon.

For all that he relished the antique luxury of his office, Judge Kushner had never even once tried to hide his humble beginnings. Indeed, he bragged about them. He used his story to inspire Miami-Dade high-school kids on career day. He endeared himself to his underlings with his homey manner—a sort of all-by-my-own-bootstraps, American-Dream enthusiasm. He charmed Miami's upper crust with the easy admission that all this—a wave of a hand to indicate his home, his marriage, his model-beautiful sons, his career and, possibly, his very self—were made real through his union with Celeste (née Farrow) Kushner, daughter of Randall Farrow, clay mine magnate, now deceased but go try to find a brick building that went up anywhere along the whole Jersey shore any time before 1966 that didn't contain clay from the Farrow-Pennsy Mining Corporation.

Also, the truth was that Judge Kushner loathed his home. Gables Estates had been Celeste's idea. She had worked tirelessly with the architect to incorporate all of the features—the his-and-hers get-dressed-in closets, the temperature-controlled wine cellar that was twice as big as the whole apartment the judge had grown up in, the koi pond off the master bedroom porch—her dream home had to contain. She had spent so many hundreds of thousands of dollars furnishing the resulting twenty-two rooms it physically hurt her husband to think of the final tally. She had been the one who'd insisted that of course one needed eight bedrooms and nine baths for a family of four.

Kushner hated the place. It was too damned big —you never knew where anyone else was in those echoing halls and were forced to use an intercom to find out if your wife was in the kitchen or the living room or out by the pool. Also, the house was too damned white—white carpeting and white sofas and flowing white curtains at every expanse of window—and he was not allowed to dip in it. Which he thought was quite small of his wife, this edict she'd handed down. He had, after all, given up his beloved after-dinner cigars on her account. Or, at least, he'd let her think it was on her account—no matter that his Dunhill lighter had gone missing and the whole smoking ritual just wasn't as satisfying somehow after that loss, she refused to accept the sacrifice had been made on her behalf.

And Celeste could not abide his filthy habit of chewing any more than she could abide what she called the stench of his lovely cigars. Years ago, when they'd first moved into the Gables Estates place and Celeste had laid down her law about his Copenhagen, the judge had weighed his options. Go home at night to a house that was too big and too bright and too filled with people from whom he grew more distant each day, or stay in his cool office cocoon where he could chew to his heart's content?

Judge Kushner never had to stop for coffee in the mornings any longer. Barbara, his secretary, had bought him the spittoon within weeks of the Gables Estates move, as she saw him spending more and more time at his office. He'd loved the gift but was reluctant to use it until she assured him that she wouldn't mind emptying it at the end of the day and keeping it clean. The judge knew that his secretary had had a crush on him since the day she began working for him, in 1983. He tried not to take advantage of it but, when she was insistent as she had been about the spittoon, he was hard-pressed not to accept her good will. One night, back in—oh, it must have been '87? '88?— well, he had had an awful argument with Celeste, and Barbara had been insistent... Such a lovely mistake, and right over there, on his office sofa...

Though, clearly, a mistake, of course.

Neither he nor Barbara had been indecent enough to even speak of it afterwards. They'd had to work their way through a couple of awkward years, of course—two people didn't, in the blink of an eye, return to a productive working relationship immediately after one of them helped the other to break his wedding vows—but they were much older now and, the judge believed, comparably wiser. He couldn't imagine the idea of having sex again with each other would cross either of their minds these days.

Still, he was going to miss her when she left— she had been making noises about retirement for almost a full year now. He was not looking forward to the process of finding another secretary—and training her; after almost thirty years together, Barbara knew her job better than he did. He, himself, however, was never going to retire. Why was one expected to retire from a job one loved and was good at simply because he had hit some arbitrary natal milestone? Retirement wasn't for people who were tired of the game, it was for people who had never understood how to play the game in the first place.

This was the truth, too: the judge's wife had long-ago spent her way through everything she had inherited from her parents. She'd gone through millions. And what did they have to show for it? He'd asked her that once, back in 2006, right after he'd forced her to show him her bank records and confirm his suspicions. "What do we have to show for it all, Celeste?"

It was as if Celeste had anticipated that one day her secret spending sprees would be exposed and she'd prepared for this very query. "We have two healthy sons and we have provided them with exceptional educations."

Which was true. Nate, the elder, had skated by during his undergraduate years at Harvard, Dad's alma mater, of course, and received his diploma in... Judge Kushner couldn't really remember his son's area of concentration. American History? There had been some talk of law school, keep following in the old's man's footsteps and all that, but it had never amounted to more than the sum total of the conversations they'd had about it. The younger one, Perry, had completed a full year at Emory Medical before he dropped out of his post-graduate degree. Now Nate was twenty-eight years old and worked for a pool service, and Perry was soon to enter his twenty-sixth year on Earth and his second year without gainful employment. Nate talked vaguely about going into broadcasting, though such talk tried the judge's patience as Nate apparently believed that getting a job as head of development at a major TV network was an entry-level thing, done as soon as he had the time to put together a resumé. Perry talked about going back to school to become a massage therapist. They both lived at home, of course, in their boyhood rooms, worked out hard at least once a day in the gym in their wing of the house, and doted on their mother so, no matter how aggravated Kushner himself might become with their prolonged adolescence, those boys weren't going anywhere.

But other than that, other than a few college degrees that, considering how they were being put to use were of no more value than the paper they were calligraphied on, what did he have to show for the few million that had passed into his hands through marriage—and right through his fingers? Not the house—that was mortgaged into what felt like infinity. Not the cars—they were leased. Not the clothes on their backs, as the bills for the credit cards that had been used to purchase them crept ever more quickly toward what were not, at the outset, ungenerous limits.

The loans they'd taken out on the house worried him the most. Then, little more than a year ago, in 2008, when the housing market tanked and the house he was living in went so deeply under water he thought he'd touch bottom, the possibility of... of losing his home... The idea had hit home that he, too, could be homeless.

Not that the Kushners would ever be, truly, homeless in any traditional sense. They'd always be able to buy a three-bedroom bungalow in some nice subdivision. But if they lost the Gables Estates house—and no matter if they did, it would be almost solely on account of Celeste's terrible management of her parents' estate—Celeste would never let him hear the end of it. He might survive a move to less posh suburbs, and it might even do the boys some good to be taken down a notch, but it would kill Celeste. And she, in turn, would make his life a living hell for the rest of its natural span.

It was only then, only under such great duress, that he began to entertain an offer a loud-mouthed ambulance chaser named Jessie Coulter had made to him months earlier.

In all the decades that Judge Errol T. Kushner had presided in Miami-Dade County Family Court, he had taken pride in the detail of his review of each and every case that came before him. Divorces, child custody cases, deadbeat dad (and a few mom) hearings. Delicate rulings around mental health issues—combing through the consequences of committing an adult to involuntary treatment. Or of not committing him. The routine of probate hearings and the assignment of guardianships for the physically or mentally incapacitated. No matter the issue that came before him, Judge Kushner wanted more than merely the facts; he wanted the case contextualized, evidence that made the case and evidence that destroyed the case; and he wanted to put each piece of the evidence on the scale and weigh it according to not only the law, but to the laws of humanity.

Sometimes—not often, but, still—he would even accompany a social worker on a home visit before he ruled on child custody, or show up for a surprise visit to a nursing home before assigning guardianship.

These days, unless some compelling counter-argument jumped out at him after a cursory reading of the documents in the manila folders Barbara handed to him daily, guardianship over those who were elderly and infirm, and who had been left with no legally-designated caretaker, were, on the whole, rubber-stamped to Jessie. Of course, the judge had to strike some balance; there were other attorneys in town who wanted a share of what Jessie called "free money"—the fees a legal guardian could, quite legally, skim to hell and back from the estate of a sick person who was alone in the world. The judge had to throw those other attorneys a bone from time to time—and once in a great while he'd have to throw a substantial bone to a lawyer who got squeaky about a particular case—but he made sure that Jessie got the bulk and/or the best that came before him, at least until his own nut was met.

The nut was eleven thousand a month.

If his work with Jessie brought in at least eleven thousand a month, he could keep treading water. Combined with a few small assets he'd saved from Celeste's long run at inadvertent liquidation and his salary, he could pay the interest on all that he owed. If, however, his work with Jessie brought in more than eleven thousand, he could put something against paying back the principle.

If his work with Jessie brought in nineteen thousand a month, he figured he might be out of debt by the time he was dead.

So far, he'd been working with Jessie for just under a year and he was averaging around thirteen a month in kickbacks.

He was never going to retire.

He was never going to be able to retire.

It was at that point, when he'd reached the mouth of despair, that he opened the manila file Barbara had prepared for Elmer Collier. He paged through it with growing excitement—Elmer was a very wealthy vegetable with no living family. If he made it for only another year, under Jessie's stewardship, with certain recommendations for fee structure, the judge would earn enough to... He scribbled a few calculations on a piece of the custom stationary in the top right-hand drawer ... He would earn enough to retire a substantial chunk of his own mortgage.

With the flourish of the plain Bic ballpoint—black ink, fine point—that the judge preferred, Elmer Collier became Jessie Coulter's newest client.

Chapter 26

My phone started to ring again almost as soon as Pablo and I had disconnected. "Yes?" I clicked through without checking who might be calling me.

"Clint Kennedy?"

It was a voice I didn't recognize. I held the phone away from my ear to check the number—a local exchange—and switched seamlessly into my officious office manager persona. "Who may I say is calling?" I had been tracked down by so many of Eddie's friends and clients and colleagues, contractors and real estate agents and every other high-rent escort in town, all of them wanting to express their shock and sense of loss to someone who seemed to be in charge. Who could give them more details that would help them to make sense of the tragedy. Who could tell them what they might do to enhance the celebration of Eddie's life that was scheduled to take place that evening at Club Boi. Who could tell them where to send flowers. I wished I had thought to add "In lieu of flowers, donations should be made to the Miami AIDs Project" to the invitations. Would have made my life over the last few hours much easier, but I had never had to plan a funeral before and Mr. Kline from Fortney-Kline had failed to provide appropriate direction on this point. And I didn't think I could relive Eddie's final saga for one more person that day without losing my mind.

"It's Ted Moses, Clint."

Among those who had called to grieve, to speak aloud about their admiration for the deceased, his loyalty and his love for life, and to confirm that they would be attending Eddie's final party, were local attorneys and judges, physicians and politicians, one police captain, one pro football player, two rival Miami-Dade real estate developers, one civil engineer, and, now, an FBI agent.

"Oh, Jesus. How are you, Ted?"

"I'm a little concerned about this evening, to get right to the point."

"Oh?" Jack waved the tequila bottle at me. Did I want another shot? I held my hand up—maybe ... "Does this have to do with Eddie's memorial party?"

"You're damned right it does! Do you have any idea of the people who will be attending this blow-out?"

"I sent about three hundred invitations, and I've been getting RSVPs all day from people—"

"From people who assume you're going to have some of the same sense of discretion that Eddie had! I want to plan on being there myself but, Clint, what the hell are you thinking? You've made no arrangements for security." He spoke as if he were an aggrieved parent whose child had failed to plan ahead for study time and failed the test.

And he was right. I had dropped the ball so hard on this one I could hear it thudding to the floor.

It was not like me to be inattentive to detail. It was the Big Picture I'd neglected. I am not a public figure, and, even so, keeping a low profile is part of both my work and my nature. Why had it gone over my head that no politician or pro football player wants to get caught at a party whose guest of honor is his side piece? Even if said guest of honor was dead.

Or, especially if.

Part of the problem, I realized, was that I continued to think of Eddie as a kid. A party boy who'd once needed my help to buy a car. In the years that had passed since I'd seen him, he'd grown to be someone I had never known. He'd grown up. Into someone who was beloved and trusted. And more self-sufficient than I would have, at one time, ever thought possible. The waste of his death rained down on me anew. I gasped and fell back against the sofa cushions.

Jack waggled the bottle of Patron at me. I shook my head. "Ted, what do I do?"

"You get me a list of all the people you sent those invitations to. Four copies. I'll pick them up if you tell me where. I'll scare up a couple dozen of our retired guys I know down here, put a few of them at the door checking names, letting the friends in and keeping the paparazzi out, scatter the rest inside to watch the temperature—do you have a budget?"

"How much do you need?"

"Fifteen ought to do it. Twenty at the outside."

"Thousand?" I put my hand down and waved it at Jack: pour—you can pour me more tequila now. "That's hefty, Ted."

"Yes. It is. You want to compare it to the cost of the lives that will be materially altered if a photographer from the *Herald* gets into that club tonight?"

"Point taken. Pick up the lists from the Fortney-Kline Funeral Home. I'll call Mr. Kline and ask him to have them ready within the hour."

"The party's supposed to start at nine—I'll meet you in the front lobby at eight, so we have a little time to get my guys organized."

"Thank you, Ted."

I heard him make a dismissive *ppffft* on the other end. "Don't mention it, man. I told you, I'll be at the party too. Self-preservation is a powerful motivator."

Chapter 27

THE judge was leaving the office earlier than usual this evening, Barbara noticed. She looked up from her desk in his outer office, away from her computer screen when she heard the door to his inner sanctum squeak open. The judge emerged in his shirt sleeves—a starched, white, Brooks Brothers button-down—rolled up to his elbows, his suit jacket draped over one arm and an armload of case files in the other.

"Barbara, this door," the judge complained, waggling it back and forth so it made a series of sharp, snappy squeaks, like a puppy was being tortured.

"I know, I know! I'll call maintenance again."

"Oh, forget about maintenance. Pick up a can of WD-40, I'll fix it myself."

"Of course, Errol," she cooed, knowing she would do no such thing. Let him dig a can of lubricant out of his four-car garage and bring it to the office himself if he wanted the door fixed so goddamn badly. In the meantime, she had grown fond of the noise; it was a head's up that he was coming or going and her job required her to keep close tabs on him.

Lest some law enforcement officer needed a warrant late at night, or that sort of thing.

"Where are you headed off to so early tonight?" she asked as he approached her tidy desk. She had worked for the judge for over thirty years and she could put her finger on paperwork from a case that had been adjudicated in his first week on the bench in less time than it takes most people to find the other shoe on the bottom of the bedroom closet. She had a reputation for her pristine paperwork—social workers and court clerks and public defenders telephoned her all the time to check their own accuracy. "Barbie Byte" her colleagues had begun calling her back in 1993, when no one but she could fathom the intricacies and nuances of the new computer system the county had installed. She had long been the courthouse's designated, if entirely self-taught, IT person.

The judge, on the other hand, had never made the switch to digital. He preferred that his cases were written up and run off on good, old plain white copier paper and handed to him in a binder. Barbie Byte wasn't even sure her boss knew the password to log into his own email account, let alone into the electronic files she maintained on his cases. Dutifully—patiently—Barbara made sure the paper files were as complete as the ones on the department's hard drive. The two filing systems didn't get updated simultaneously. Not all the time. Filing actual paper took so much more time—the folder had to be located in its slot in the right cabinet drawer, then the right location for new information within the semi-chronological order of the file had to be determined, then the paper needed to be punched and prongs unfolded and papers slipped off and on and off and on the prongs, and then the file had to be folded closed again and replaced in its slot...

"I'm going to a party," the judge told her. "I wanted time to go home and get a shower and a change of clothes first—"

Barbara felt her heart muscle tighten. What fucking party would that be? Over the years, she had watched the judge head off to countless parties—cocktail parties, dinner parties, bar association fêtes, Republican party fundraisers, opening nights for the Miami Symphony, and Parent-Teacher Night at the boys' school when the boys were still young enough for that sort of thing. Every event had chafed at her weary devotion to the judge, knowing, as she did, that his wife would be accompanying him. Celeste Farrow Kushner, the girl who won the prize though she had nothing to recommend her except her father's money. Except for Mr. Farrow's millions, Errol certainly would never have remained married to that chic, distant cow. "What party would that be?" Barbara asked brightly.

The judge laughed. "Nothing that would interest you, I'm sure. A bunch of men getting together for a... a wake, I suppose," the judge stuttered. Errol T. Kushner was not a stutterer; he prided himself on the stentorian clarity of his voice when he issued his rulings, and the halt in his words caught even him off guard. "A wake, of sorts, I suppose."

Well, thought Barbara, that was a relief. "Whose wake?" she chirped before she noticed the tenderness of the gaze the judge was aiming off into some more appealing middle distance.

The judge shrugged his shoulders and collected himself. "No one you'd know."

"Oh, now..."—Barbara spoke as she accepted the stack of files the judge was handing over to her—"don't sell me short. How long have I been working for you? I know everyone you know, surely, by now."

The judge looked at his secretary, his head cocked in genuine bewilderment, like an old dog who doesn't know his master is about to take him out to the back forty and put him out of his misery. "I can't imagine that's true," the judge murmured and, then, to her, "File those, would you? And let the lawyers involved know which guardianships have been assigned, get these estates settled. What do you say, Barbie, we make a bet we can have all existing estates out of probate by the first of the year?"

"I think that would be a lofty goal, Errol," she replied, and giggled at his optimism.

"And, still," he said as he slipped into his jacket, "a goal."

"And so I will do my part," she promised, "as always. Though my hope is not as large as the task you've set."

"That'll do," the judge assured her, and winked, as he opened the door to the hallway and let himself out for the night.

Barbara watched him go, smiling, hugging the stack of files he'd handed to her. "Son of a bitch," she grinned.

She sat the stack on her desktop and opened the one on top. Barbara was a disciplined, methodical worker—it was one of the reasons she was such a genius about the order of her paperwork; everything she did was top to bottom, left to right, out of her inbox and right into the outbox without interruption of another task. Stay focused, touch each piece of paper only once, put one file away before you pick up another.

The first file in the stack belonged to the Liddick case—Mrs. had been in an extended care facility for nearly a decade when Mr. had a heart attack and died. Three kids and seven grandkids, four of them adults, all of them living out of state and not one of them willing to travel to Florida and look after their mother, now that she was left alone. Barbara wondered if the kids were ungrateful snots or if Mrs. had simply been such a bitch none of her kids wanted anything more to do with her. She went back and forth between the scenarios while she waited for Sherri at Dan Marakovitch's office to pick up.

"You've reached the office of Dan Marakovitch, attorney at law," Sherri answered, "how may I help you?"

"Hi, Sherri, it's Barbara at Judge Kushner's office," she said, and moved her hands to her computer keyboard, opening a new email template, typing quickly.

"What do you have for me?"

"Go ahead on Liddick, I'm emailing you the signature page now," Barbara said, and hit send. "Check your inbox."

The second in the stack belonged to the Guerrero custody case, assigned to the public defender Frank Bathurst, and the third belonged to the Neiman divorce, with a copy of the final decree to go to the attorneys for both parties. Barbara handled both these cases efficiently, filing the folders in their appropriate slots in their assigned drawers.

The fourth in the stack was, again, a conservatorship case. It belonged to the Collier estate. Barbara opened it flat on her desk and then scooted her chair back on its rollers so she could reach into the bottom drawer of the cabinet directly behind her desk. From the drawer she lifted a solid sheaf of paperwork, maybe thirty or forty pages of it, and she sat that on top the file. She took care with the paper punch, aligning carefully the two holes she'd need at the top of each sheet to make the pages fit neatly on the prongs inside the existing file case.

When the pages were all properly punched, she removed that day's notes—a measly two pages—from the prongs and placed the sheaf that had been sent from Xavier Sousa's office earlier in the day in its proper chronological order in the folder.

Then she replaced the more recent notes, as well as a freshly punched sheet bearing the judge's signature, on top again.

After composing an email to Carla at Jessie Coulter's office, she dialed her up.

"Jessie Coulter's office," Carla answered.

"It's Barbara at Judge Kushner's office. How's your day, dear?"

"Oh, Barbie, you know"—Carla was discreet enough not to pass on news of the hullabaloo that had erupted around Ethel Nestor—"same old same old. Whatcha have for me?"

"Go ahead on Collier, I just emailed the signature page to you."

"Collier? Really? Jessie said, naw, he thought there was a guy in Mexico was supposed to have the conservatorship on that one."

"Well," Barbara said, "I don't know about that, do I? I'm not the judge, I only see his signature telling me to go ahead and give this one to Jessie, and it's a big one, Carla, so you'd better get on it. An old man with dementia out in Sunshire, and three houses the deceased was flipping and work on 'em won't stop until Jessie decides the best way to liquidate, you know?"

"Hey, I'm not going to argue. Jessie will be happy."

"That's what we aim for, isn't it? Everyone happy!"

"Thanks, Barbie."

"My pleasure, Carla."

Barbara stowed the Collier file in its proper drawer before she turned her attention to the fifth in the stack. "Son of a bitch thinks I'm going to retire and he can just replace me? Thirty-six years together and he thinks he can dump me that easily?" She spoke out loud, and then she laughed. "Thirty-six years together and Errol Kushner thinks he can send me off to the pasture while he stays on top of the dung heap, Mr. Important Judge with the fancy wife and the fancy house and the fancy parties? Well, we'll just see about that, Errol Kushner. We'll just see about that because you are *nothing without me. Nothing!*"

Barbara realized she had raised her voice. One of the things that she had learned in her years as the office manager for a busy judge was discretion. People—social workers, defendants, prosecutors, private investigators—flocked to her to try to garner insights into the judge, how he might rule in their case, or how he was inclined to rule, and what they might do to impact his thinking as he was deciding how to rule. It was mostly subtle stuff, the things these people did—cheerful phone calls, baskets of goodies from the patisserie at the Fontainebleau, and, in one case, an orchid plant, a purple Pleione, that she had managed, against all odds, to keep alive for going on three years now. They all just wanted to be on friendly terms with Judge Kushner's office and, when it came right down to it, Barbara Anne Clifford was his fucking office. She took several deep breaths to enable her to return to a whisper before she once again opened her mouth. "You just try to be whoever it is you think you are without me, Errol Kushner.

See how easy that is. Son of a bitch. See how that works out for you."

Chapter 28

I was irrationally irritated that Pedro had not, of course, packed a tux for me in the duffle bag I'd asked him to throw together when I left Mérida for Freeport—the morning I first learned David had had a stroke. That had been just a few days ago, but the days had been so compacted with stress it seemed I had been living with weights and worries stitched to my shoulders for months at that point. Why would it have even occurred to Pedro to throw in a tux? On that long-ago morning when I'd set out for the Bahamas, he might as easily have packed lederhosen, as a tux was a costume I thought I'd need just as urgently.

So now I stood inside of Jack's closet, before a cupboard of evening wear. Missing was the full white tie regalia of the sort I knew for a fact David kept in his closet, but there were half a dozen dinner jackets, all in sparkling white, in fabrics ranging from linen to light-weight wool, and as many styles of tuxes—a Calvin Klein with satin peak lapels, a Gucci with notch lapels, and an Armani with a shawl collar. All in black, of course, except for the Tom Ford in navy blue. A row of shiny patent leather shoes, from oxfords to loafers, sat beneath the rack. There were velvet boxes containing sets of studs in a narrow drawer and, in the drawer beneath that, a chromatically-arranged display of bow ties. At least a hundred bow ties, some with matching cummerbunds.

"Whatever you want," Jack said and waved an arm, permission for me to wear whatever was in his closet so that I would be appropriately clothed at Eddie's memorial party that evening.

Generous of him, certainly, but the problem was that Jack's a good two inches shorter than I, and my back is broader; whatever I chose was going to look too small for me—no, it was going to *be* too small for me.

"Here's me with my own plane and I didn't think to dispatch it to Mexico in time to bring me one of my own tuxedos." I sighed.

"You should probably keep at least one tux in your condo here," Jack advised, "for just these sorts of emergencies."

I thought about that. "How do you know you're a rich guy?"

Jack frowned back at me. "How?"

"You have formal wear emergencies."

Jack snorted. "Clearly you haven't figured out how to be one yet."

"A rich guy?"

"That's what I'm saying."

Likely he was entirely correct, I thought, as I pulled out the shawl-collared Armani.

An hour later, Jack was pulling his Porsche into the parking lot at Club Boi. The sun had set, and, from the outside, the club was completely dark. Anyone would have thought we'd pulled up to an abandoned building, except for the gathering of solidly-built, serious-looking men all dressed in black suits around the entrance. I spotted Ted immediately—he was standing behind a podium at the head of the line, shuffling through the copies of the guest list I'd provided with three or four of his hastily-recruited security team; Mr. Kline was consulting with another team member about the configuration of the red velvet-rope line.

"Go ahead in," Ted called to me. "I'll meet you in about ten—we're almost sorted out out here."

From the outside, with all the old FBI guys in their dark suits milling around, the club might have looked as if it was not opening for business that evening, maybe hosting a private gathering of Mafia types. Or vampires. Inside, it was filled with the controlled chaos that usually precedes a damned good party—fifty or more people moving and chattering with speed and purpose: bartenders, not yet shirtless, polishing glasses and stocking coolers, tapping kegs and cutting lemons and limes; caterers billowing white cloths on banquet tables, setting up chafing dishes and lighting sterno, in the case of the Mexican spread; chefs at the raw bar and sushi station filling ice bins, preshucking oysters and sharpening knives; maintenance crew members on ladders hanging disco balls, gold metallic streamers and white lights from the rafters, or on the ground wiping cocktail tables and sweeping the floors; dancers, not yet stripped down to gold lamé costume, who would fill the six gilded cages placed on pedestals and strategically located around the room, stretching out in between the cocktail tables, warming up; Dr. Dack's road crew setting up his amps and turntables and sound board, and Dr. Dack himself testing a mic: "One, two, testing. One, two …" When the sound levels satisfied him, Dack boomed, "How about we all get ourselves in the mood for a party?" and dropped *Boom Boom Pow*. I heard his laugh echo in the mic as he watched all of us on the floor in front of him, watched our postures change in the nanosecond the music began, watched us all begin to dance in spite of any other job we might also be engaged in doing. One bartender whipped his bar rag around his head now as he worked. The chefs' knives sliced to the beat. The dancers threw their backs into it. *I'm on that supersonic boom, Y'all hear that spaceship zoom… Boom, boom, boom…* The bass overload seemed to be conducting itself through my bones; the tensions and sorrows of the last several days shut down, like notes I'd written to myself being folded and tucked away in a safe place in my brain, easily retrievable when I had to deal with them again tomorrow but, for tonight, out of sight. I could feel my shoulder muscles loosen, and begin to sway.

"Does anyone have an easier job than you do?" I asked Dack as I danced up the two steps to his stage.

"I don't believe so, Clint." Dack is taller than I am by a good six inches, and I am not short. He also has the build of a gym rat who works out nearly obsessively. His head is pristinely shaved bald, and his teeth—except for one shiny gold incisor—are brilliant white and look huge against his deep-cocoa skin. "You in charge of this circus?" he asked as he embraced me in a hug that a man much smaller than I would have considered stifling.

"I am." I reached into the jacket pocket of Jack's snug tux. "Your check, sir." I extended to him the envelope I'd extracted.

"You have got to be kidding me," he said and, instead of taking the envelope, shook his hands at me as if I'd just offered him a fistful of garden snakes. "You know who was the guy told all the club owners to hire me back in the day? I know you know that was Eddie. Tonight is my gift to him."

I was caught off guard but not really surprised. "That's really good of you, Dack."

"Thought the world of the boy," he replied. "Least I can do."

Chapter 29

A N upturned garbage can, as it turned out, was the perfect height to elevate a leg. No need for that special stool Carla had wanted to buy; why waste the money? No need to see a doctor, either. The knee was impressively swollen, but Jessie could still walk on the leg, albeit with a limp, and he could even bend it almost to his butt, if he moved slowly and carefully enough, without grunting in pain. He had a supply of hydrocodone in the medicine chest in his little office powder room—expired now, he saw when Carla brought him the bottle, but then expiration dates were really nothing more than a marketing ploy anyway—and Carla was punctilious about keeping him on a steady ice/heat/rest rotation. She had a plastic bag of ice cubes in the freezer compartment of the half fridge and an old sock filled with rice that she heated in the microwave: what more could he ask for?

"A cup of coffee, Carla. And a donut. Go next door and get half a dozen. Take the money out of petty cash. Get glazed."

Any time Jessie got loose with the petty cash, Carla partied: "Live a little, I'll get a whole dozen!" she shouted to her boss as she made her way to Dough-Ray, the donut shop that shared a wall with the offices of Jessie Coulter, Attorney-at-Law, in the potholed strip mall off West Okeechobee Road.

"A dozen," she called as she opened the door to bells chiming. The bells let Ray Milano, always in the back tending his ovens and deep fryers, know that a customer had arrived, and Carla's shout let him know what size box he should bring with him to the display counter.

Carla eyed the sparse leftovers from this morning's labor. She thought that any other donut shop owner would have donated the couple of dozen pastries left at the end of the day to a homeless shelter or a food pantry and gotten the hell out of there to spend time with his family, or just in front of the TV with a cold beer. Not Ray. Ray did all right—Dough-Ray's was a go-to breakfast stop of sorts for Floridians in-the-know—it wasn't as if he was hurting for money. But Ray's day ended when all of his donuts were sold, not before—though he had been known to knock off with a few eclairs or scones still viable. On those days, a customer could find, the next morning, a small selection of day-old wares for half price. "Two chocolate-topped, two crullers, two strawberry-filled, that one bacon maple there"—Carla pointed—"and five glazed."

"What's the splurge?" Ray asked her.

"Got his knee banged up. Sugar's the best medicine," she answered, handing him a twenty.

Ray rang her up and handed her back her change—forty-four cents in coin and a ten-dollar bill.

Carla curled her hands and rested them on her ample hips. "Don't you know better than that by now?"

"Right. Sorry." Ray returned to his cash register and changed the ten for a five and five ones. Carla crumpled the Dough-Ray receipt into a ball and tossed it into the trash can behind the counter, folded three of the ones into her bra and the rest of the change into her fist.

"Ya know, Car, it ain't like going to Office Depot to get copy paper and paper clips. He knows how much a dozen donuts cost from me."

"Yes, I know he does. I also know he has no patience for bookkeeping. As long as he's cashing in somewhere near to what he estimated in his brain would be coming in, he leaves the numbers to me. A couple, three extra bucks a couple times a week and I can fill up my gas tank on him, cheap bastard. Wouldn't even think of doing it if he paid me a decent wage in the first place, you know?"

Ray allowed that he did, and then he smiled as he watched her turn from the counter to head back out his front door. Carla had been tricky about it, but Ray was sharp: he hadn't missed the four copper pennies she'd slid out of the need-one-take-one dish by his register as she'd turned to go.

"Glazed have arrived," Carla sang as she bustled back through the doors of Jessie's offices.

"Can't exactly waltz out there to get 'em myself," Jessie sang back at her.

"On my way," Carla answered, dropping her fist-ful of change into the petty cash box in her top desk drawer and stopping to make a cup of coffee in the office Keurig on the way.

Jessie knew what Carla was up to in their tiny office kitchen; he knew why it was taking her so long to make him a cup of coffee. If he could walk comfortably he'd probably catch her right in the act of stuffing a few of her favorite flavored Keurig pods into her pocket, or shoving a few rolls of toilet paper into her handbag. He always knew when she was running low on toilet paper at her house because she'd come in carrying that god-awful neon-orange, over-sized tote she had.

It surprised Jessie that it didn't bother him she stole from him. It was always the smallest things she took, and even he knew he didn't pay her enough for her—often very competent—skills. He'd even thought, once, about giving her a raise —something beyond the token COLA-inspired pit-tance he provided at least every other Christmas season—but he hadn't acted on the impulse. He'd realized in time that even if he paid her twice the salary she was currently drawing, she would still steal from him. And from Ray over at the donut shop. And from Citizen's National when she did the business's daily banking—in this case never money but pens and calendars and pads of sticky

notes and, years ago now, the industrial doormat upon which clients of Jessie's legal practice
still wiped their feet. Stealing Keurig coffee pods
and rolls of toilet paper from him was Carla's own
little thrill. He would never take that away from
anybody. A couple of times she'd taken things of
more substance from him—his cell phone charger
cord, a pair of argyle socks gone missing from the
pocket of his going-to-court suit jacket hanging
on the clothes tree in a corner, his Kiwanis pin.
But he'd long ago discovered her Christmas box
stash so he knew where the items were located,
if ever he found himself with a desperate need of
them, so he let the pilfering of even those items
go.

Still, right now, he was immobilized behind his
desk, and his own cash box was sitting open in
his lap. He'd been counting out the week's payroll—Carla, a couple of PIs he kept on retainer
—and worth every penny, Kushner; as he heard
his secretary moving through the kitchenette, he
stuffed the piles of counted money on top of the
cash box drawer, slammed the lid and slid it into
the desk drawer where it lived. Carla knew that
drawer was where he kept his cash box, locked in
a locked drawer because, though he truly doubted
anything with a value over five bucks would catch
her magpie eye, why tempt?

"Here you go," Carla trilled, placing the cup of
hot coffee on a napkin before him. She danced
behind Jessie's desk, put the donut box on top of
the credenza and opened it up. "Shall I serve?"

"I can reach."

"That's all then?"

"You want a cruller?"

"That would be lovely."

"Take it then."

"Don't mind if I do." She took a bite before she added, "Barbara called."

"What'd we get?"

Carla grinned. "Elmer Collier."

"Get out."

"Nope, it's yours. Downloaded all the paperwork just before donuts."

"Huh," Jessie grunted, pleased with the windfall and still surprised. "I thought they were looking for that Mexican guy, you know, they had a guardian for him? Thought that case was off the table."

"Well"—Carla shrugged sadly—"you know how it goes. People don't always want to be bothered. And why would someone who lived in Mexico agree to look after an old guy in Florida in the first place? Probably felt guilty so, you know, in the moment he said he'd do it. Probably thought better of it after."

"Probably decided it wasn't worth the headache?"

"That's what I'm saying. Just easier to turn the whole thing over to a pro!"

"You got the file?"

Carla scurried out to her desk and then right back into Jessie's office. "Ask away. What do you want to know?"

"Assets?"

"In the range of two million."

"Say it again—"

"In the range of two million."

"Where's the old guy?"

"Sunshire."

"You'll take care of getting him moved out of there?"

"Before I leave for home tonight. But there's one other thing you ought to know. The guy's grandson, the kid who was killed so Elmer doesn't have anyone anymore? He was a house flipper and he's got three in the works over in the Grove—"

"Jesus Christ," Jessie bellowed, "I'm not a fucking contractor. Tell 'em stop, stop all work." He shook his head and looked heavenward: God, this is supposed to be free money, you know, so why did it always seem to come with so much work attached? "Anyway. I'll make a few calls, see if I can get someone who knows what he's doing in to look at the places. Tell me the best plan for liquidation and then you better say your prayers, Carla, that it doesn't include having to supervise a house renovation because it'll be you driving out to fucking Coconut Grove every day."

He wished he was walking right. He wished he could follow surreptitiously behind Carla as she waddled out of his office, cruller in hand— he had pissed her off and now he knew she was going to have to do something pissy in return. As soon as she got out of the office door, out of his line of sight, she'd have to turn around and stick her tongue out at him, or give him the finger, or maybe she'd just crouch down and practice her twerk outside his office door. He wished he could catch her in the act—that always made her turn twelve different shades of purple.

He listened to her trudge down the hallway, heard when her footsteps stopped, waited for the squeak squeak squeak of the subfloor that told him she was on the other side of the wall twerking at him right now. When it came, he burst out laughing.

"What?" Carla called to him, her response so instantaneous, and oh, so innocent.

"Not talking to you," Jessie called back to her, still chuckling. He leaned back in his chair, reaching to the credenza for his first glazed. "I think I'm gonna need some more heat for this knee pretty soon. Aren't I about ready for heat again?" he asked, and sent Carla scurrying before he settled in to enjoy his donut.

Chapter 30

I drank champagne. A mid-priced bottle, considering that I'd had to lay in over ten cases for the event, but something I wouldn't have been ashamed to serve at my own dinner table either. I let a waiter fill my flute, clicked it against Jack's to toast Eddie, and then raised it high in tribute to him as Dr. Dack faded out the music around 9:45 PM and took a moment to welcome the revelers, to point his own flute at the dark-maroon cloisonné urn that sat on a pedestal near the stage, safely distant from the roiling dance floor.

I danced with Jack, and Xavier, and Ted, though Ted was more interested in supervising the security measures he'd put into place, and I think the only dance he shared all evening was with me.

I danced to Lady Gaga and Wolfgang Gartner and Vanessa Amorosi belting out "This is Who I Am" like the final frontier of personal liberation and felt, for an hour or so, as if I were fifteen again and exploding with the hormones that made a kid take the sentiments of this sort of pop-angst so to heart.

I drank vodka. Poured ice cold into a martini glass that had been sprayed—oh, so sparingly—with a mister of vermouth, garnished with a plump Spanish olive stuffed with a slice of pimento.

I danced with a stunning group of Miami's top escorts, about nine or ten in all, every one of them an alum of the service I'd run—oh, so many years ago: Josh, a bodybuilder, hulking and ripped and more graceful on the dance floor than one might suspect of him at first glance; Oliver, an ethereally beautiful young man, half-Japanese and half-African-American, who supplemented his escort earnings by modeling, mostly, so far, for local resort brochures, and one J. Crew catalog; Leo, a student at Florida State while in my employ, now a draftsman for an environmentally-conscious construction firm, who couldn't quite yet let go of the glamour and easy money and exuberance of being an escort.

I danced to Lolene, huddled in writhing reunion with my former employees, as awkward as anything the singer had ever had in mind and as much fun as "Sexy People" deserve.

I drank absinthe. A single shot I'd drenched in sugar and icy water from a silver-plated fairy fountain.

I danced with people I didn't know, with people whose names sounded vaguely familiar and like I should know them, with people to whom I had just been introduced—a surgeon who worked with Laine Gordon at the Ryder Trauma Center, and a judge who sat on the Miami-Dade Family Court, and an honest-to-god Miami Dolphin.

I danced to Cascada and Madonna and Kaci Bataglia, dancing ever nearer to the urn on its pedestal as the evening turned into night and the crowd that wanted to get down swelled. I swayed at midnight, while the lesbian witches conducted their rhythmic incantations, and bounced around as gleefully as anyone else among the riotous crowd as the white balloons came down on our heads, and leaped to allow one of the hired dancers to grab my hand and pull me up for my own turn in a gilded cage—to wild applause, I might add.

Even so, I was still functional enough to break from the crowd to check on Eddie, to enlist one of the roving waiters to help me move the whole display another ten feet back, right up against a back curtain so there was no danger of Eddie taking a spill on the dance floor. It was then I noticed the mass of envelopes that had been laid at the base of the urn, some tucked by their corners under it.

I opened one—a condolence card and, tucked into that, a check for five hundred dollars made out to the Miami AIDs Project, to be donated in Eddie's name.

I opened a second—a check for a cool thou.

A third—another five-hundred-dollar check.

I picked up all the envelopes, making a stack, counting their number as I tidied them up: forty-one checks in total; I estimated that, at minimum, I held in my hands twenty thousand to benefit the Project and I decided, right in that second, that, whatever the total, I was going to match it before I made the donation.

I took the stack of envelopes and found Jack. "Go lock these in your car, will you?" I handed the stack off to him. "Donations in Eddie's name, and I suspect there'll be more before the end of the night, but I don't want to leave twenty thousand just sitting on a pedestal near the dance floor."

"Roger that," he replied, as I went back to drink and dance.

Chapter 31

Wednesday, October 28, 2009

THE next morning, I awoke in my condo, on my sofa, to my cell phone blasting a summons, my throat parched and my thigh muscles spasming in pain. I was no longer used to the sort of intense drinking and dancing I'd indulged in the night before. I massaged my legs amid fuzzy memories of attempting a Russian kick dance sometime around three AM, as I headed toward my kitchen hoping there was a can of Coke, or Sprite, or anything carbonated and non-alcoholic in my still pitifully bare fridge.

"Oh, thank fucking god," I muttered at the lone can of Coke beaming like salvation on the second shelf. I popped its top and guzzled half the can before I realized that, while I was naked from the waist up, I was still wearing Jack's too-tight Armani tuxedo pants. I'd apparently unzipped them before I'd passed out, and now I peeled them down my legs and stepped out of them and left them on the kitchen floor while I went in search of my cell

phone, on the quest to still the incessant summons.

"Yes," I gasped into the phone.

"Good morning!"

"Go to hell, Jack."

"That bad, huh?"

"Let's just say...," I paused and popped three
Advil, washed down with the rest of the Coke, "Eddie will remain on my mind for the rest of my life
after last night, because that's how long it feels
this headache is going to last."

"Well, then, you're going to love this part: Mom
just issued the order for a command performance.
We're due in their kitchen for brunch in forty-five
minutes."

"Your parents are indecent people. What time is
it?"

"A little after ten."

"Oh, fuck. How did it get to be ten already—"

I dialed Tim while I was in the shower, put him on
speakerphone. "I was worried when I didn't hear
from you first thing this morning," he said when
he picked up. "It isn't like you not to call to check
in on a new schedule, which went off without a
hitch, I know you're waiting to hear that. We're
all good here—" he assured me, and then paused.
"I mean, except for, well, a few people, you know
who."

I did. Emiliano and Felipe, and more than a few
of their soldiers. I still had no idea what was happening in Mexico, or why—and I had no desire to
know, except in that it would have been a comfort

to know at least which side of this apparent war Pablo was on, offense or defense, and was it the winning one.

I dialed Pablo as soon as Tim and I had clicked off, but he didn't pick up. I debated about a message and settled on a quick, "Call me when you have a minute," and then brooded about why he wasn't answering his phone the rest of the way to the Cohens'. Pablo *always* answered his phone— or, he *almost* always did and his increasing inaccessibility was beginning to spook me. And, surely, this morning, when he'd asked specifically for assurances about the Tamaulipas pick-ups— which I could give him if he would just answer his fucking phone!

I bumped up the Cohens' driveway, ground my car into park, and stepped up to the front door under Candace's arbor of climbing roses. The door was standing open, which had not been unusual in the summertime when Abe and Jack and I had been thoughtless boys and Candace had to constantly admonish us that she wasn't paying to "cool down the whole gawddamn state," though it struck me now as out of the ordinary.

Until I heard the cacophony inside the front door: nothing like the normal hushed bustle I expected at the Cohens', the maid and the gardeners shuffling efficiently around busy people living their lives. Even the addition of David's nurses as he recovered added little volume to the natural, low-key cheerfulness of the Cohen household. What I heard now were ear-splitting squeals followed by aggressive, theatrically evil laughter, followed by a young, female, Spanish-inflected voice calling out, "Dawna, no, you come back here! Nathan, you stop chasing your little sister!"

I made my way, with terrible trepidation, toward the back of the house. I saw a bad moon rising at 11 AM Eastern Daylight Savings Time. I found, in the kitchen, among the usual suspects, one boy child and one girl, genders discerned from the way they were dressed, but pure Pugsley Addams and Butch from *The Little Rascals* from their comportment—without question, spawn that could have issued only from the elder brother of this house.

"Abe's kids?" I asked, feeling weak on my feet, forcing myself forward and lifting my hand to greet the nanny the children were huddled around, introduced to me as "Elinda". "Good to meet you, Elinda."

"Sharon had them out-of-state, I don't know if you knew that?" Candace was addressing me as she shooed the nanny, who in turn shooed Abe's kids outside to play. "I told her I wanted my grandchildren living in Florida, where I could see them regularly, and I wanted her to bring them for a vacation, to see us in Freeport in the meantime, and that little tart told me I could *have* the damned kids if it meant that much to me. And then she told me exactly how much it would cost."

"So," David chimed in, "as soon as we got home, Candace got Xavier working on it, and we bought our grandchildren!"

David, I was happy to see, was looking more robust—pink and animated—than I'd seen him since before Abe's arrest.

I knew, however, that until he was well enough to get himself out of that house and/or its new residents, Butch and Pugsley, were well past the squealing stage of their young lives, my visits with him were destined to be few and short.

Chapter 32

CANDACE served me a Bloody Mary, which she divined I desperately needed, and coffee all around. While the maid and the nurse worked around the island, cooking up gluten-free pancakes and turkey bacon—what Candace allowed David to eat was, apparently, what she was going to allow any of us to eat, for the duration —one of the gardeners popped in and dropped the morning newspapers on the table in front of us. David reached instinctively for the *Wall Street Journal*, and I think it was only Jack who saw my face turn ashen at the headlines that stared back at me from every other newspaper in the pile: DEA agents crowing about their third raid within the week, the forty-two smugglers killed so far, in their 'fatal crackdown' on drugs at the border, this one in Nogales, Arizona, on the border of Sonora, Mexico. The raid had taken place in a barn on land owned by an Arizona rancher, an American citizen. I couldn't easily find an indication in any of the coverage that the rancher was not among those considered smugglers, or if he survived the raid, but that was Matias's territory and I had no doubt that Matias was now, himself, no longer among the living.

The result of what was surely being cast as a completely separate incident.

I barely made it through brunch at the Cohens' table, was barely able to swallow the texture-less pancakes, covered, as they were, with a sugarless fruit compote and not a bottle of maple syrup any-where to be found. I excused myself shortly after the maid cleared our plates, before Candace could refill my coffee cup. "Heading off so soon, Clint?" she asked.

"Yeah, I have a few things to do this afternoon. Make hay while in Rome—"

Candace cocked her head. "Still a little too hung over for a coherent metaphor, I see," she said, but she let me go.

I was in the car for a good two and a half sec-onds before I had it peeling out of the Cohens' driveway in reverse and Pablo's line ringing on my cell. When, for the fourth time, Pablo's line went to voicemail, I pulled off on Krome Avenue so my hands could stop shaking.

What did all these raids add up to? Was Pablo orchestrating them, as I'd supposed? If he was not, who was? And why were the heads of the various branches being taken out along with the sacrificed soldiers? And did any of this mean that Pablo himself was in danger?

What would that mean for our laundry busi-ness, if Pablo was in danger? Out of favor...

Would that mean that I was out of favor now too?

And how far—given that he'd already banned me from returning home until he gave me permission—would Pablo go to protect me? *Could* he protect me? *What the fuck had I done that I would need protection from?*

I needed to do something that would take my mind off these dire thoughts. Had I been in Mérida I would have driven to my school and further complicated Miguel's life with more tweaks and revisions and expansions to the school's construction plan. Upended the serenity of the head master I'd hired, a former New Jersey state public-school administrator who'd lost his wife and kids and home to divorce when he'd lost his job to alcoholism. His resumé had arrived on the day I'd set as my deadline to hire for the position and it seemed like an omen to me—at least, in acknowledgement of his excellent timing, I owed the sender the courtesy of looking at it.

The man's resumé—Darius MacGinniss's resumé—was as impressive as any that had so far been submitted to me. And his references were excellent, with the exception of the last school that had just axed him. I'd dialed his phone number on a whim, and he'd picked up. "Why do you think the job at my school in Mérida is a good fit for you?" I'd asked him.

"I sent that resumé packet to you on the day I came home from rehab. I believe a new locality is critical for me to successfully continue the program I'm on, and why shouldn't the locality be a beautiful, warm, healing place in Mexico? Nobody ever got better in New Jersey, believe me."

He laughed sardonically. "Also, I need a hard job, preferably in my field, to give me the store of self-esteem I think it will take to stay on the straight-and-narrow. Frankly, Mr. Kennedy, I need some-one who's willing to give me a second chance."

I am a sucker for second chances.

So far, not Miguel nor Tim nor anyone else had reported any untoward incidents back to me—and, make no mistake, I had my spies out on Dar-ius; trust but verify. Darius was working out well for the Aj Tz'ib Academy, except for one crucial thing: Darius required a reliable routine under-taken in a pacific ambiance. Not counting the kids themselves acting up—which Darius dealt with quite admirably, in fact—I was the primary source of unrest in his life. I knew he was exas-perated by the notes I left for him to find on the mornings after I pulled my all-nighters. The way my flights of fancy disrupted the curricula he'd devised or the budgets he'd assigned to specific programs. I couldn't yet make the former public-school administrator comfortable with the idea that cost was not my primary concern for any program or alteration to it we might undertake at Aj Tz'ib. And so, if he didn't reach that comfort level soon, I wasn't sure that he would work out in the long run.

The ordinary balm of my school wasn't available in Miami, of course, so I did the next best thing; I drove to South Miami, to the demolition site of our newly-acquired branch building. See if there was a distraction there that would somehow ab-sorb me until I could get Pablo to pick up his fuck-ing phone so he could clear me to go home.

The demolition site was depressing—tons of 1970s pre-fab trash headed to the town landfill, a mass of ugly waste twisted and stuffed into a series of dumpsters parked at the front curb. I looked at the lot, the wreckage it contained, and tried to imagine a fresh, new bank building in its place. It struck me, then, as I tried to get a sense of the architecture of it, that perhaps I should talk with Jack before we did any more work on this site. Rethink the purpose of investing more into the purchase. What if the things that were going on in Mexico were going to change our business model—and impact our profits—in ways we couldn't possibly anticipate with the information now at hand? In that case, would we still want to build a new branch in South Miami? Would we be able to afford it—not just the new building itself, but staffing it, and operating it? I quickly formed the opinion that Jack and I needed to look at our projection calculations and P&Ls, and reassess what we wanted out of South Miami—in light of the different scenarios that could now be unfolding south of the border—before we solidified plans for this now-vacant lot.

Then I noted the building that stood, like a debauched debutante, right next to our vacant lot. It was an Art Deco ghost, one that had spent far too much time in purgatory, but it was easy to see past that—or it was easy for *me* to see past that exterior, and smile at the bone structure of the place. I walked up to it and pulled my handkerchief out of my back pocket so I could wipe a window, where a sheet of the brown craft paper, taped up from inside to block of the view of nosey people like me, had fallen away. I gasped at the original, wide-plank hardwood floors, and at the brass gas jets that protruded from above the wainscoting. What if, I thought, what if, instead of building a new bank, we bought *this* building? Renovated *this* building into our bank? The lot on which the old one stood could become a parking lot, and accommodate a drive-through too, but the actual bank could be something magnificent... if we located it in this historic old dump.

Just the thought of taking on such a renovation cheered me up considerably. It gave me a sense of both satisfaction and promise—and, I wondered, if our Mexican adventure came to an end, was it possible that Jack and I had built the bank into an institution that wouldn't flounder without the drug lords? Were we doing enough business, without Pablo's contribution, to go totally legit? Could we afford to do that at this point?

And still afford to be able to renovate a new bank building in South Miami?

And still be able to afford supporting my school in Mérida?

And still not mourn the loss of all the millions that could have been ours if only we'd had the *cajones* to stay the course?

Adrenaline had been spurting through my brain in chaotic but frequent doses for days—would I /could I give that up? Could I go back to a life without the ready, steady flood of cash, or the delicious element of fear always trickling right along the edge of the deluge for me to dip into it?

Chapter 33

THE bottom line was that I wanted to go home.
I *needed* to go home. I missed my house, the
good life I had in Mérida—mornings with my feet
dangling in the cool pool on my patio; a wide circle of friends who appreciated good food and good
wine as much as I did—albeit most of them were
drug lords; the ease of the relationship I had with
Pedro, who could, for all intents and purposes,
read my mind.

And I missed the hell out of my school. I don't
think I'd realized until this point how much I de-
pended on that project to give purpose to my life.
Or at least give me something of value to use to
fill up the copious downtime I was supposed to be
enjoying these days.

I needed to sit down with Pablo and tell him to
give it to me straight, because the limbo I was living in was torture. Were things going south down
in the south? And, if they were, would I ever be
able to go back to the life I loved living down there?

I left the bank site ping-ponging between despair at the thought of the laundry business going belly-up, fear of what folding up the business

might mean for my personal safety, and, aston-
ishingly, a real spark of excitement at the idea of
taking on a brand-new renovation—a new project
into which I could toss all of my excess energy and
adrenaline. I drove straight to the neighborhood
where Eddie's houses were located. Maybe throwing myself into choosing floor tiles and countertops for the flips would act like a steam valve...

Given my state of mind, I was more disappointed
than surprised when I got to the cul de sac and
saw that no work was taking place at any of the
three locations. Total quiet, and all of the doors
locked up tight. No crews were hanging drywall or
replacing old windows or removing chunks of old
sidewalk concrete.

Even in my funk, I was self-aware enough to
understand that part of the reason I'd driven to
the flips—perhaps a larger part than I understood
at the time—was the hope that I would run into
Charlotte on site. But, of course, she was among
all the other people who weren't there either.

I had, in the moment, no suspicions that work
on the houses had been actively called to a halt.
The idea didn't even cross my mind. What I did
think was that work crews here in Florida were
no better than the ones I dealt with in Mexico. If
you weren't on top of your project every single day,
then they weren't either. Here was the primary
rule of any renovation project, whether you are
meticulously renovating a graceful, old Colonial
in Mérida, Mexico, or lipsticking a two-bedroom
bungalow in the Miami suburbs: everything takes

longer than you could possibly anticipate. Contractors, in the kindest interpretation, are piss-
poor time managers. Oversight can turn into a
full-time job, but shirking on it is not an option.

Also, the corollary: everything costs more than
you've budgeted.

I sat down on the top step of the concrete porch,
just above the walkway Charlotte had helped to
dismantle, to bask in my foul mood and figure out
my next move. Which was, of course, to put aside
whatever it was I could not control and concen-
trate on those things I could; I just had to work
through the bulk of my irritation before I could
return to a rational train of thought. I had pulled
my cell out of my back pocket and was scrolling
through my contacts list to find the number for
Eddie's contractor, when I got an incoming call.

From Pablo.

I refrained from shouting "Where the fuck have
you been?" into the phone when I picked up.
"Pablo," I sighed. "It's good to hear from you."

"Did you doubt you would? Hear from me?"

I looked heavenward. "I read the papers."

After a long pause, Pablo asked, "And you are
worried I am in some danger?"

I paused too, before I spoke. "I would like to
come home."

"Of course," Pablo said. "Perhaps in a week or
so, I think."

I knew that no good could come from arguing
with him. "OK."

"Good!"

"Pablo? It isn't an unreasonable worry, in light of things. Is it?"

The pause this time was so long I was on the brink of asking, "Pablo? Are you still there?"

"You called me fourteen times in the last few hours only to tell me you are homesick?" was what he eventually said.

"No. No, I didn't." But damned if it didn't take me a few seconds to remember what I had been calling him about. Another of Candace's eye-opening Bloody Marys would not have been un-welcome. Even just another cup of strong coffee. "Abe," I blurted at last.

"The one in prison."

"Yes." But that was all I could say. Now that I had Pablo on the line I didn't have a clue how to phrase either my news, or the request I had to make of him. I had no idea the kind of code that was required in these sorts of situations. "So. Abe. He is the"—I tried not to choke on the word—"*beloved* son of two of my American partners, who would be devastated if anything ever happened to him. I mean, *anything*. They are very attached to their son."

"As you could say of most parents," Pablo prod-ded me along, though I didn't know whether to be comforted or alarmed at his observation.

"Yes, well, his father, who loves his son, wants him to sign certain papers—family matters, noth-ing that involves anyone outside of the family. But, well, he's refusing to sign the papers and that's a problem. Also, he's always been, you know, jealous of how well his brother and I have done in life, and sometimes he says crazy things …"

"Such as?"

"As… as in that he would arrange to make trouble for our businesses. Though," I hastened to add, "I doubt he could cause much trouble. From prison. You know?"

I heard Pablo laugh, the first time I'd heard that sound in weeks, a soothing sound even if I knew full well he was laughing at me. "No, Clint. Not from prison. He could not cause much trouble from there."

Chapter 34

THURSDAY, October 29, 2009
First thing the next morning, a sultry Florida Thursday, Jack and I were back in his Porsche, headed once again to the Miami Federal Correctional Institution. This trip was the result of a frantic, early morning phone call, placed collect to Candace, from her son, Abe.

The call had upset Candace deeply, as demonstrated by the free-flowing tears she shed just after dawn, when she summoned Jack and me to her home and told us about it—as demonstrated by the raspy whisper in which she delivered her information to us, lest David also hear what Abe had conveyed and become as agitated as she was by the news. My first thought, as I listened to Candace cry, was *leave it to Abe to be unable to handle what had happened to him with any sort of grace. Leave it to that big baby-man to go crying to his mommy when his nefarious plans went awry.*

On the other hand, I reasoned, he had just lost a finger—the pinky finger of his left hand, specifically—and I suppose I'd be royally put out about that too. If you put aside the fact that I'm too smart to try to cross a cartel boss in the first place.

As Abe told it—sitting across from his brother and me at a small table in the visitor's room later that morning, his left hand wrapped in gauze, his body and voice still shaking well after the fact, as thoroughly chastised as it was possible for a human being to be—he had been innocently standing in line outside of the Mod One bathrooms, waiting his turn to take a morning shower, when two large men butted in line in front of him.

He'd seen these two around the prison before, but they had never been part of the cell block social circle he was forming, and he had never before seen them in his Mod, which rang a small alarm bell in his pea brain. That bell—that subtle warning signal—had prevented him from bitch-slapping them out of his way. That, plus the fact that one of them was Hispanic and the other white and one rarely saw individual members of the different prison tribes band together as real friends, and these guys were talking together, possibly even exchanging jokes, in fast, amicable Spanish. Also they really were so much physically larger than he was. Abe said he put his head down and didn't protest that they had jumped the line. And then the two goons began a conversation with him.

"Brother, don't you think what I say is true?" the white one asked.

Abe said, "I don't speak Spanish, so I have no way of knowing."

"Oh, Brother," the Hispanic one said, "we are just saying that it is very wise for men to tend their own houses first, before they make notice of another's house."

"For men to keep their own noses clean," the white one added.

"For men to keep their fingers in their own pies and not put them into another's food," the Hispanic chimed in, as if it were now a game of metaphors, and Abe really wasn't following in any case except then, as he laughed at his own observation, the Hispanic goon threw his weight against Abe and pinned him to the wall, and the white one grabbed Abe's left hand and, in the next nanosecond, caused him to feel the most violent physical pain he had ever before even feared experiencing. He heard a metallic sound—garden clippers, like Mom uses on her climbing roses, he would think later—and his empty stomach cramped and shot a wad of burning bile up his esophagus. His knees grew so weak he was almost glad for the goon pinning him against the wall, keeping him from sliding to the floor in shock.

In the next nanosecond, before Abe could even think about trying to shake loose of the white goon's grip and inspect the source of the mind-blowing pain, the Hispanic goon breathed down on him—"This is just one finger, but you have nine others we can use to keep teaching you lessons if you put them where they should not be. You understand?" But he did not wait for an answer. The goons let go of him and vanished quickly among the morning crowd.

Abe had shouted, "Fuck!" and then he'd brought his hand to his face, which caused a searing pain to zap like a lightning bolt from his palm to his shoulder blade, and he saw the stump where his pinky finger had been just moments before. The blood pumped from the wound and dripped to the floor and onto his rubber shower shoes. The cry that escaped him then was such a loud, pathetic wail that every other inmate in line for the showers turned to look at him in time to see his eyes lose focus, his face go slack, and his body thud to the floor.

"We had nothing to do with this," Jack told his brother, and I knew, in his mind, this is what he wanted to be true.

Abe knew better. "Don't fucking lie to me, man," he blubbered, lifting his gauzed hand and using the thumb to rub the gauze around his head—he'd sustained a gash over his right eye when he'd passed out on the bathroom floor, a gash now held together with seven stitches and miles of sterile wrap around Abe's big head. "Just don't lie to me," he repeated and used his good hand to pick up the ballpoint pen Jack offered him. He let it hover over the documents Jack had pushed in front of him. "When I sign this, we're all good, right?"

Jack nodded, but I felt it prudent to take advantage of our position: "Your mouth, Abe. Don't meddle in other's people's business. Don't even talk about it."

I saw it cross his mind—the possible punishments that might be meted out to him were they to object to his lips as well as his fingers—and I knew that Abe would think twice before ever again even uttering his brother's name, or mine.

Jack tucked the signed documents in between his seat and the console and steered us away from the Miami Federal Correctional Institution. "I don't know," he said as he merged onto Krome Avenue, "if my mother will ever get over this."

"I know."

"*They cut his finger off!*"

"I know."

"I don't know if *I'll* ever get over it," Jack spat at me, as if the mutilation were my fault.

Or, my fault *directly*, though I knew he had a better understanding of our business arrangements than that. The idea that I could have prevented Pablo from taking care of our problem in his own, inimitable way—let alone ordered it to be done—wasn't what was on his mind. I was convenient and he needed a whipping boy.

"Fucking *cut his pinky finger off!*"

Frankly, I wasn't sure *I'd* ever get over Abe's missing digit either. Alvaro's murder, the assassinations of Emiliano, and Felipe, and, probably, Matias were of a different order than a finger unceremoniously sliced from someone you'd known since childhood. Even if that someone was as much of a lifelong asshole as Abe Cohen.

"Are you losing your stomach for this business?" I asked Jack. Because it was easier to ask him about his shaky nerves than to own up to the fact that mine were fucking twerking all over my body.

"They. Cut. His. Finger. Off," Jack repeated.

"I know," I said. I did not add, still, he's not *dead*.

A fact for which I was grateful.

But I knew better than to call Pablo and thank him for small favors.

Chapter 35

I drove aimlessly around Miami, not sure at all that I'd know what I was looking for if it jumped off an overpass and landed on the hood of my car. I thought of my plane, languishing in a hangar at Miami-Opa Locka Executive Airport. I'd been so eager to fly it back to Mérida, cruising in my own Gulfstream back to the life I had loved. Still loved. People I cared about. Pedro, the Mayan kids, Miguel, Darius, Tim. Even Pablo.

Especially Pablo.

Not that I didn't have people in Miami I cared about too, of course; the Cohens were family. But if I was going to both leave Mérida and continue pulling my weight in the family business, the bank, then that was going to entail a whole lot of days—like, five a week—putting on a suit and tie and getting to an office by nine AM. I would probably never lose the habit of industry, but I had so long ago left the corporate world that I was no longer suited to it. Or, at least to its hours.

Not to mention—and forget about the fact that Abe's missing finger had me so shaken my insides were still rattling around as if they were in a mosh pit—how did one extract oneself from a cartel? How did one leave this sort of business? Was it possible to leave such a business, or merely impossible for *me* to do so, while still alive, because I was now in too deep? How did one even begin a conversation about a career change with a drug lord? It wasn't that I was scared of Pablo in the ordinary, day-to-day scheme of things, but I was fully aware that he could arrange a hell of an exit interview if he was disinclined to my voluntary resignation.

These dark thoughts assumed that there would even be a business in Mérida to go back to. There was warfare going on a few miles south and I hadn't a clue about why. Or about which side was going to emerge from the rubble, largely because I had no idea who the two sides were. I knew only that it wasn't the cartels against the DEA. And that the DEA was the useful fool for whatever housecleaning the kingpins were hoping to accomplish. As far as the housecleaning itself went, however, I didn't know how the kingpins were aligned on whatever controversy had made the mess, or who might or might not be aligned with Pablo, or if Pablo himself was going to survive the sweep. I knew only that three of the kingpins had already *not* survived it. Forget whether I wanted to stay in my position, job security was not a foregone conclusion.

And then I thought about my plane again and realized that I'd been so sure I'd be returning home any day now, I'd kept Amelie on call for four days straight. Which was a cruel oversight; the girl deserved a glass of wine if she wanted one, so I called to tell her it was unlikely we would be going anywhere until at least the following week.

"Then there's a guy I want to call back and accept his dinner invitation," Amelie said, "hang up so I can."

I laughed and clicked off. One good deed, and it made me feel nice to know I'd made her happy. Not that anything—certainly clearing the calendar so my pilot could have a dinner date—was ever going to make up for Abe's pinky finger and make me feel like a good person again.

Jack had dropped me off at my condo as soon as we'd returned from our visit with Abe, and I immediately jumped in my car and went off to do something—anything—to keep thoughts like that out of my head. So far a stop at CVS to pick up razor blades and a trip through the Starbucks drive-through weren't doing it for me. I steered with one hand and used the other to go through the recent call list on my phone.

"Tim."

"Hi, Clint."

"How's the day so far?"

"Boring."

Boring was our inelegant code for uneventful and, thus, without problems worth comment or concern.

"Great," I replied and hung up.

I worked my thumb down the scroll again and pressed a call. It went to voicemail. "Hi, this is Clint Kennedy, about Eddie Collier's properties?

I was by yesterday but you weren't—none of your crew was. We need to set a meeting to talk about your work schedule. If these properties aren't your priority, I'd like to know so I can look for another contractor. Call me back so we can discuss."

I clicked off and worked my thumb one more time. "Damn it," I muttered as the call also went to voicemail. "Hi, I'm calling for Lisa Winder. It's Clint Kennedy. I worked with you when I bought my condo earlier this year? I'm interested now in a property in South Miami. On Red Road. It's the one immediately adjacent to a newly vacant lot— my company just tore down the old bank building that had been there. I'd love for you to arrange for me to get inside. Thanks. Call me."

My thumb twitched, in anticipation of another scroll, but then I realized I was driving aimlessly in the direction of Sunshire so, rather than call Donna McAdam, I might as well swing by and pay her a visit.

The first time I'd visited Elmer Collier, it had been all about me. I'd wanted to reassure myself that my new charge was as comfortable as it was in my power to make him—so I could comfortably return to Mexico and not have to worry about ever again setting foot in Sunshire. And it had been about a date with Laine because in my sex-addled brain I thought... What? That a visit to a nursing home would make me seem like the sort of sensitive guy she'd been waiting for?

Christ.

Maybe it was my own latent humanity finally kicking in—or maybe it was the horror of what had happened to Abe's pinky kicking my humanity in the ass—but I needed Donna McAdam to know that Elmer Collier was not alone in the world. I would certainly not be in to visit him every day, but I would know what medications he was on, in what doses, and for which ailments. I would know enough to be more than the old man's legal contact, the first person to call when he kicked; I'd be his advocate while he was still with us.

Donna McAdams eyed me through the windows to the reception area, from the safety of her desk. I have, as I've noted, exceptionally well calibrated people-reading skills, but I didn't need them to interpret the look on her face: I was an unexpected and unwelcome interruption. I expected to see her, as willfully as necessary, change her facial expression to one of undiluted delight when she caught my eye, but she didn't. She glared at me for a few seconds, and then she got up slowly and sauntered to the receptionist's desk. She kept the desk between us and offered her hand only when not taking the one I had stretch out to her would have been unforgivably rude.

"Hi, Donna. I'm sorry if I'm catching you at a bad time. I can come back later if that'll be more convenient?"

"Why do you need to come back?" she asked, and her eyes narrowed.

I physically hopped back in surprise. "Because I would like to talk with you about Elmer Collier."

Donna shook her head. "He was moved first thing this morning, and all the paperwork is in order, he was signed for—"

"*Signed for*? Dear God, did he die?"

"No, he did not die! Although I can't think it did anything good for his fragile constitution to have had him moved!"

"*Then why was he moved!*"

Had he had a medical emergency? A new ailment that required more specialized care? Or, oh, fuck, had I screwed up without even knowing it —had the bank withheld a payment while Eddie's estate was sorted through the courts? Certainly no nursing home would be so cruel...

Donna stepped back and put one hand over her heart. "I have no idea. When I walked into work today I was presented with a court order from Mr. Collier's guardian, transferring him to Seaside Gardens." Her eyes narrowed once again. "You are his guardian, Mr. Kennedy."

"Well, yeah, that's right, but I didn't have anything to do with a court order. I was happy with him here—"

"I certainly got that impression when you visited us—"

"I had no reason—"

"I thought it had to do with costs, of course, Seaside Gardens is much more... economical—"

"Yeah, cost isn't a problem, the old guy's loaded. Look, there's been a terrible mix up here, I think —"

"It would seem." Donna eyed me again with her slitty cat eyes. Clearly I was not to be trusted with responsibility for Mr. Collier, not if I could lose him in my first seventy-two hours on the job.

"This is not my fault," I insisted. "But I will find out whose it is. And I'll have it put right"—I almost grabbed Donna as the thought occurred to me— "You still have his bed open, right?"

Donna offered me her next words grudgingly, for Elmer's sake, not mine, two hard little turds: "I do."

"Good. Keep it open. Until I get him back here. Tonight, I hope." Each phrase had seen me inching closer to the door, but I paused. "Meantime, this Seaside Gardens? It's not a bad place, right? Not the worst place for Elmer to spend a few hours?"

Donna exchanged a look with the receptionist before she spoke. "It's a shithole," she said.

Chapter 36

I sat in my car in the parking lot at Starbucks, sucking down my second Venti Latte of the day, amped up on caffeine and adrenaline. I glanced at the cell phone resting on my thigh, waiting for it to ring. My instinct had been to drive directly to Sunset Gardens and take Elmer back to Sunshire myself. My better judgment intervened, fortunately; how was I going to move an unconscious man and all his various life-supporting equipment? Stuff him into the trunk of my car?

And barging into Sunset Gardens and demanding that they move Elmer right back to where they got him could get me the top spot on the Daily Florida Nutcase Register, which would be —let's face it, this being Florida with its hordes of nutcases—some sort of degraded accomplishment. At least it could if there was some sort of real legal glitch about who was and was not the man's guardian. I decided to give Xavier time to look into whatever clerical error had triggered this awful mistake. I wanted to have a leg to stand on when I marched into Sunset Gardens, and I waited impatiently in my car for him to call me back and give it to me.

"Good news?" I greeted him when my phone finally rang.

"Well, depends on how you look at it."

I rubbed my eyes with my free hand. "I can't handle cute right now, Xavier. Just tell me."

"Well," Xavier said, "seems that Judge Errol Kushner assigned Elmer's guardianship, as well as the management of Eddie's estate, to a lawyer out in Hialeah—a fellow named Jessie Coulter, whose practice it seems, in the majority, is managing the estates of the elderly who are incapacitated but have no heirs." He added the editorial comment: "Must be a booming business—it is Florida, after all."

"But why?" I jumped in, right to the point. "Why would this Kushner guy do that? *I'm* his legal guardian. I never gave any indication at all that I wasn't ready to step up and do my job."

"Clerical error, as you've suggested. I think that's all it is, Clint," Xavier said. "Nothing that can't be put right."

"Yeah, maybe to you and me, and to Kushner and Coulter, but let's think about the trauma to Elmer, of moving a dying man halfway across the fucking city, and now having to move him back? How do we explain that taxing little outing to him?" I demanded.

"Clint," Xavier said gently, "he's not even conscious. He slept through the whole thing. Elmer is likely the guy least impacted by any of this."

I rubbed my eyes so hard they hurt when I stopped. "I don't like you much right now, Xavier."

"Yeah, so, then you'll probably actively dislike me when I make this next suggestion, but I think you should hear me out and consider what I'm saying."

I drained my paper coffee cup. "What?"

"If you let this stand—if you let Jessie Coulter take over the management of Elmer, and Eddie's estate, if you let that happen—you're off the hook." I made a pained sound and Xavier began talking more quickly, over my objections: "Clint, I know Judge Kushner. He's a good man, not the type to give over the care of the elderly to someone who doesn't know what they're doing. He'd only deal with someone who knows the state system and how to get the patient the best care, and knows how to conserve an estate's money, and—"

"Jessie Coulter moved Elmer into a shithole!" I wailed. "That's how he saves an estate money, by putting the patient in a shithole, and I wonder how much fucking money he's really saving any estate, what the oversight process is for finding that out, because, I have to tell you, Elmer's dying … but he could live to be a hundred and still have enough money to keep him settled in a fucking gold-plated nursing home. How much of the difference between the costs of a good nursing home and a shithole does Coulter put in his own pocket? Does Kushner get a cut of that?"

"You've become very suspicious in your old age, Clint. Coulter's a member of the state bar, there are standards he has to live up to, and Judge Kushner is simply *revered*—"

"Jesus, Xavier, listen to yourself! You've become very naïve in your old age, but I have no patience to debate that with you. Just…, please, can you take care of this? Can you do whatever it is you need to do so I can get Elmer back to Sunshire. Tonight? So I can get him back to his home tonight?"

"I can put in a call to Kushner."

"Thank you," I said and felt better for about two seconds. Until the next logical thought flitted through my brain—"I'll bet that's why there's been no one working at Eddie's flips!"

"Jessie Coulter shut down the projects?"

"That's what I'm thinking."

I dialed Eddie's contractor as soon as Xavier and I hung up, but my call went straight to voicemail. Again. I punched my steering wheel—and then I got what struck me, in the moment, as a brilliant idea.

I sped to Homestead, the neighborhood where the Cruet house stood, the tiny bungalow that Charlotte shared with her father, the Cohens' longtime gardener, Chester. Chester Cruet was a solid, compact man of more than sixty years, with the sort of permanently tanned, leathery skin you'd expect of someone who'd worked outside in the Florida sun for nearly half of his life; he looked plenty older than he was. He'd come to the US with his family as part of the Mariel boatlift, the mass migration of Cubans to the states that happened back in 1980. In Cuba, at one time, he'd been an in-demand landscape architect. In the US, he'd met David Cohen when he answered Candace's ad for a head gardener at the Cohen estate. Candace had given him work he was far too qualified to have, and David had become his friend, helped him launder the fifty thousand dollars he'd smuggled out of Cuba and secure a mortgage to buy the bungalow I stood before now.

I hesitated at the front gate—what the hell was I doing?—but momentum propelled me forward and up the three concrete stairs to the front door, where I knocked hard, quickly before I lost my nerve.

Chester answered my summons. "Hello, Clint."

"Hi, Chester."

Both Chester and I were at a momentary loss for what to say to each other next. He knew me through the Cohens, and the stores of affection he had for David and Candace ran deep; he wanted to welcome me as a fellow intimate of theirs and, so, as a friend. On the other hand, the last time I had stood at this front door, I'd come to force his daughter's hand, to convince her to turn herself in for the crime of conspiring to rob the family bank. It was the right thing to do; for Charlotte, I mean. I saved her jail time by getting her to turn on Abe. In any case, Chester was an old-school Cuban patriarch—his word was his bond and, he'd repeatedly assured me during the trial, he was grateful I'd convinced his daughter to come clean—so she could confess, and repay, and earn her way back to the place where her word, too, could be her bond.

Even if it had meant crushing her dreams and pissing all over the future she'd planned to make for herself.

"I need to see Charlotte," I said. "I promise you, Chester, it's nothing bad. Not for her, anyway."

Chester sighed, but he stepped aside so I could enter his home, and he tilted his head toward the kitchen and called, "Charlotte! Charlotte, we have company!"

"I heard someone knocking," Charlotte called back and then appeared, banging through the kitchen door holding a wooden spoon in one hand and licking chocolate cake mix from the fingers of the other. She appeared so quickly that Chester and I hadn't yet had time to take seats in the small dining room, on a couple of the light maple, colonial-style dining chairs that ringed the table. "Oh," she said when she saw me.

She made me wait until she got her cupcakes in the oven. Then she came out to the backyard, where Chester had led me while she finished in the kitchen. She had a stovetop timer in her hand. "Eighteen minutes, as long as it takes the cupcakes to bake—no more, no less unless you leave first," she said. "That's what I'm giving you."

Chester got out of his chair so quickly he grunted. "I guess I'll just leave you two kids alone."

Charlotte put the timer down in front of me, on a small, three-legged, faux-wood table between the two vinyl striped lawn chairs on the concrete rectangle that passed for a patio. The timer ticked, loud and tedious, as she plopped herself into the chair her father had just vacated. "So?" she asked.

"Why were you told that work on the houses in the Grove was being stopped? What reason were you given?"

She was taken aback that I was being so direct. Giving it back to her.

"The project was cancelled," she said. "That's what they told us."

"Who told you?"

"My crew boss."

"He—what? You just showed up at the site yesterday morning, and he told you there wasn't any work and sent you home?"

"You knew that. Or you wouldn't have come looking for me here." She shrugged again. "In this market, I would have appreciated the work. But I've been with the company for a few months. I'm getting to the top of the on-call list."

I've never been bothered by moral gray areas. I mean, I launder drug money for a livelihood *and* I run a school for underprivileged kids—I am a walking, talking gray area. Right at that moment I was torn between asking her if she had learned her lesson and was done being stupid, and apologizing to her for forcing her into confessing her crime and bringing the law down on her. As always, however, when I was around Charlotte, rational thought and normal human emotion were plundered by her angel face. Her perfume of roses and fresh-cut pine. Her bright smile. Part of me was ready to do anything whatsoever within my power to dissolve the scowl on her face and make her smile at me.

"I have a question for you, Clint," Charlotte said.

"Yes... anything."

"How come you're involved? How come every time I get fucked over, you are somehow involved?"

Chapter 37

IT was too late for lunch and too early for dinner when I arrived in Xavier's office, but he took one look at me and bundled us both up to the French restaurant he'd caused to be built on the top floor when he'd purchased the tower where his offices were located in 2007. The restaurant was supposed to be a vanity project, for Xavier's personal convenience, the garlicky escargot and steak au poivre and Cotes du Rhone he could not seem to live without just an elevator ride away whenever he wanted to entertain clients or craved a snack. It had turned into a destination spot for clued-in Miamians, discerning tourists, and people who wanted to suck up to the great Xavier Sousa—there was no signage at ground level, and the place had never paid for even one newspaper ad or one radio spot; and it certainly did not have its own Facebook page. It was the sort of place you had to know about to access.

When Xavier and I walked in, it was empty except for one batch of waiters tearing down the dining room after the lunch rush and another batch resetting it back up in anticipation of the dinner crowd. Xavier steered us toward the bar and the incoming bartender was at our elbow before our butts could hit the black leather seats of the Eames-inspired barstools. "I know you're closed right now, Art," Xavier said to him, "but I have a friend who could really use a martini right now. Two Tovaritches, up and dry, please."

"Yes, sir," Art replied.

"So?" I asked as the bartender scurried to prepare Xavier's order. "Have you heard from your boy, Kushner?"

"I have," Xavier said. "Or, anyway, I've heard from his office. The judge's calendar is full today, but his secretary told me she'll talk to him about Elmer Collier as soon as he's out of court. She's a good girl," Xavier said of the sixty-something woman who ran the judge's office, "known for her command of details, but she offered that if there was a mix-up at the judge's end she'd make sure it was corrected."

I held up my hands. "When, Xavier? When does she plan on doing that?"

Xavier sighed. "She'll call me back first thing in the morning."

I dropped my head into my hands. "So, Elmer just cools his heels in a shithole until some clerk figures out where the t's aren't crossed and springs him?"

"What do you want me to say in response to that, Clint?"

I refrained from whining.

"Why did you show up at my office?" Xavier asked. "You could have just called. What's on your mind?"

"Other than Elmer?"

"Other than that, yes."

I shook my head. "I don't know. I'm so... frustrated. My hands have never been tied like this. People doing stupid things that are beyond my control—against my best advice— in the process making everyone's problems worse. What is apparently a clerical error keeping an old man hostage in a dump. Abe getting it in his mind that he's going to sabotage the bank from behind bars and ending up getting his finger cut off..."

I lowered my voice as the bartender approached and set before us the most appealing cocktails I think I'd ever seen—the purest of vodkas, unadulterated by any hint of vermouth, garnished with perfect, solitary, unstuffed olives skewered on tiny forks of real silver, the silver glinting against faultlessly polished martini glasses now frosting from the cold of the alcohol they contained.

Xavier picked up his martini glass by its stem. "Abe was being an idiot, as usual, and Elmer has no idea where he is, dump or not. There's your cold comfort," he said, and gestured for me to pick up my own frosty cocktail.

Which I desperately wanted to do. But what I said was, "I can't."

"Not in the mood for vodka?" Xavier asked.

"No"—I shook my head—"it's that I've been putting off going to the Cohens' all day. I have to drive over there and face Candace before the day's out or I won't sleep at all tonight. If I drink that, you're going to have to call a cab and tell the driver to take me home and pour me into bed."

Facing Candace, who'd always insisted we face adversity squarely, was the most difficult part of a rock-hard day. I'd wanted to make a little easy drug money—money so easy to come by it was almost free—and now I had to take my lumps from a mother whose son had been mutilated, in part, because of my scheme.

The mood at the Cohens', when I arrived, was strangely subdued. The housekeeper, quietly dusting the bannister of the sweeping front staircase, nodded me toward the back of the house as I entered, and she put a forefinger to her lips before she pointed it upwards; I understood to keep it down, the ailing David up there taking a nap. Abe's two impossibly unattractive children were doing their part in the endeavor, sprawled, with their nanny, on the floor of the west living room, silently sharing a Spongebob Squarepants coloring book and a Crayola Ultimate 152-pack of crayons.

In the kitchen, David's nurse, Henry, greeted me with a small smile, as if a bigger one might have been too loud in this house. She was standing at the sink, handwashing a few odd glasses. "Hello, Mr. Kennedy," she said. "They are on the patio, Mrs. Cohen and her son..."

I nodded my thanks and slid the glass door aside to join them at the glass table, which was littered with an ashtray Candace kept for Jack's convenience, a wine bucket, and their two glasses.

"Would you like a glass?" Candace asked, lifting the bottle of Chardonnay from the bucket and its bath of watery ice. "I'll ask Henry to bring another glass." I shook my head—don't go to the trouble—and took a seat with them at the table, as Candace shrugged and poured the last bit of the wine into her own glass.

"Candace," I began, "I don't know what to say-"

"Don't," Candace cut me off. She finished off the wine before she continued. "I'd like to tell you to get out, you and Jack, out of this business you're in. Get out clean, and get out now." She smiled and rolled her eyes. "But I knew as well as you did the risks of going into this line of work in the first place." She shifted in her chair and put a hand over one of mine. "I have known about the risks of Abe's shaky judgment since before he was even a teenager." She let go of my hand then. "And still, I was greedy enough that I approved your plan. So I am reaping what I have sown."

"Oh, Candace..." I whispered, looking to Jack for assistance, but his head was bowed, his eyes intent on his fingers interlaced in his lap.

Candace interrupted me, thankfully, because I still could think of nothing to say that might comfort. "David, however, will never know of this. Or, what I mean to say is that he won't know about it *now*. I suppose I'll have to tell him about Abe's... accident, at some point, but not until he's stronger. Not until he has his health back."

"Certainly," I told her. "Of course."

Candace smiled; there had never been a question that she would be obeyed.

"Also," she said, "I am terribly worried about others of my boys"—she fanned her fingers at Jack and me—"being hurt." Her eyes clouded, but she took in a sharp draw of breath and they cleared. "How one extracts oneself from an arrangement of the sort we've made—well, I have no idea, but I would love that to happen. Whatever the costs to the bottom line." She looked at me, and then at Jack, until she had caught us both in her gaze. "But not to the cost of your safety. You must promise me, both of you, that you will not be stupid."

"Agreed," I said with all haste.

"Would be hard to be as stupid as Abe, in any case—" Jack offered.

"And that will be all of that," Candace warned him. "Also, Jack, go home." This last said with much kindness, but real meaning. "Please, go home. We have all sorts of people to take care of us and it feels absolutely oppressive to have you hovering over your father, as if he really is too feeble for the ladies around here to handle."

It took Jack a moment, but he laughed. "Hey, Mom," he said, "you don't have to kick me out. I'll go happily. I have a date tonight and I'd just as soon take him back to my own place than to try to sneak him into my parents' house—"

"With the same fellow you had a date with last week?" Leave it to Candace to zero in on the important part of the information conveyed.

Jack grinned. "Same fellow."

"Well now, isn't that something?" Candace marveled. "I don't think either of you have had a second date in years," she trilled.

"That's not true—"

"Don't try to defend yourself, she's completely right about both of us," I told him.

"And a second date can lead to a third, and a third to a fourth, and a fourth to meeting your parents, and getting engaged, and..."

Neither of us interrupted Candace. She'd get to the part where Jack got engaged and married and gave her more grandchildren soon enough, whether we cut her off or she raised her voice so our objections were drowned. We just laughed, Jack in embarrassment, and me in wonder—in spite of the two trolls coloring in the living room, Candace Cohen would welcome as many of the little beasts as we were willing to provide to her.

Whenever that might happen.

Chapter 38

JUDGE Errol Kushner longed to be in a different line of work, one in which he wasn't required to even know what a burner phone was. Now he sat alone, in the driver's seat of his silver Mercedes sedan, at the side of an orange grove, deep under the cover of country darkness, wishing he had a spit cup, dialing Jessie Coulter on the burner he'd provided when they'd begun this unholy alliance.

"Coulter," he barked when the attorney picked up.

"That's my name, who's calling?"

"You know damned well who's calling." He opened his car door and spit onto the rich, dark soil. "Why haven't you returned my secretary's calls all day?"

Jessie reached behind, to his credenza. There were still donuts in the box Carla had most recently purchased. He didn't need another one, and they were a little stale, but glazed is glazed. "Maybe," he said as he bit into his pastry, "I didn't like what she wanted to tell me."

"Look, man," the judge growled, "you can't just avoid me whenever you feel like it. I made a mistake in assigning the Collier case to you. The man has a legal guardian, and the fellow is rather keen to undo whatever it is you did today—some business about moving the patient to a different nursing home?"

"To a place the patient could better afford—"

"Not as I understand the man's finances," the judge said. "In any case, my secretary—who is usually faultless about these sorts of things—mixed up the paperwork and I'm amending my ruling, putting Mr. Collier back into the care of—"

"Judge Kushner, why'd you want to do that?"

"Because Elmer Collier doesn't need a court-appointed guardian! His family made arrangements for him. He has no need of you!"

"Oh, but, Judge," Coulter cooed, "we have need of him."

"I don't have that much of a need," the judge snapped. "Do you know who's representing the guy who's contesting the custodianship arrangement? Xavier Sousa. You know who Xavier—"

"Yes, I know who Xavier Sousa is—"

"Then you might also know that he doesn't frequently stoop to dealing with family court matters —"

"Oh, the hell with the high and mighty Xavier Sousa and his rich, fancy clients who all lead lives so clean and straight they'd never end up in family fucking court. I might also know you have more of a need than you generally let on."

"And that"—the judge spat again—"is completely beside the point."

"Is it?"

"Listen to me! This is the fourth or the fifth time I've made a mistake of this magnitude in as many months. I'm worried my mind is going, Coulter, because my secretary never screws up like this! I may not ever be able to retire, but I'll be damned if I'll compound my sins and other failings with fraud!"

Jessie Coulter chuckled. "Far above fraud, are you, Judge?"

"See here!"

"Oh, see what, Judge?" Jessie leaned back in his chair and snagged another donut, the maple bacon one, not his favorite, but it would do. "Look, let me just push back at this guy, just a little bit. My bet is he backs down quick enough. I mean, the guy, this Clint Kennedy, he's a rich, young bachelor living in Mexico—what's he want with an old guy in a coma in Florida, anyway? Let me give a little shove back, see what he does."

The judge closed his eyes, and then he spit again. "I'd really rather you didn't, Jessie."

"Just, you know..."—the judge heard Jessie warble a few high, simple notes—"just a small shove, see if that gets us what we both want."

The judge still sat in his car, under cover of country darkness, by the side of an orange grove, spitting onto the rich, dark soil. He longed to be in a different line of work—one in which he and a certain shady lawyer named Jessie Coulter might never have met.

As it was, he took the crisp white handkerchief from his front jacket pocket and used it to wipe down the burner phone—to polish it as shiny as he'd had to polish his dress boots in the Army—and then he got out of his car and placed it directly beneath the left front wheel of his Mercedes. He returned to the driver's seat and turned over the engine, which seemed to him to roar in the rural silence. Then he put the car into gear and drove back to Gables Estates.

Chapter 39

Friday, October 30, 2009

IT was my expectation that Xavier would have worked out my problem regarding Elmer Collier's custodianship by morning. This is exactly why one forked over top dollar to have an attorney of Xavier's status on the payroll—because he not only knew the law, he knew the people to call to make sure the law was enforced. Sure, he couldn't roll a complicated case through the court system any more quickly than the court calendar allowed, but when it came to correcting what was certainly nothing more than a clerical error—and one that involved the health and comfort of an elderly human being—I had complete faith.

I still wouldn't say my trust was misplaced— I understood on an intellectual level why Xavier wanted me to review all my options before I fought to gain full legal custody of an old man I didn't even really know. It was on an emotional level that I was rattled: Judge Kushner had owned up to a mistake on his end and, instead of instructing him to correct the mistake straightaway and forthwith, Xavier had acquiesced to the judge's request that I first meet with the estates' attorney to whom he'd assigned Elmer's care.

I sat once again in Xavier's office, in one of the two dark-gray cashmere-upholstered chairs in front of his desk, demonstrating my impatience by drumming my fingers on it as obnoxiously as I could. I must have looked a bit better than I had the last time I'd sat here—in any case, Xavier didn't whisk me to the rooftop and have the bartender pour me some medicinal vodka; today he asked his secretary to serve us coffee.

"Clint," Xavier laid out his case when we both had cups in our hands and were again alone, "you have no connection to Elmer Collier, other than through an old employee. You have a business to run. Do you really have time to take on Elmer, not to mention all the estate's other issues—dealing with Eddie's flips, liquidating his stocks... selling his townhouse? And you live in Mexico, for crying out loud," he added, as if Mérida was the straw that would break this camel's back. "Why does this matter to you?"

"I'm not sure!" I shouted. And I really meant it. If I'd thought about it, I might have realized the thing I'd truly tripped over was that Elmer had been *moved*. I was irrationally furious about the injustice of it—why should an old man be denied the end-of-life he'd earned just so some smarmy local lawyer could skim his life savings? Where I chose to focus my mounting frustration was, however, on the mundane: the calendar. "Jesus Christ, Xavier, it's Friday! Do the people who are going to have to move him, do they even work on the weekend? He's probably not going to get back to Sunshire until Monday at this rate!"

I'd offered to go to the offices of Jessie Coulter, Attorney at Law, to meet my adversary, but he'd declined. "Why don't you let me take you to lunch?" he suggested instead. It always raised a red flag, albeit a small one, whenever someone shied away from taking a meeting with me in his own office. What was wrong with the office? Did he even have one? I had arranged to take meetings in restaurants, too, during some off periods of my life, when I had been conducting business without a home base to call my own, so my suspicions weren't completely random.

So I told him Cvi.che 105, at noon. It was pricey and Peruvian. One way or another, that ought to throw him.

I'd ordered a variety of appetizers and was already tucking into the ceviche when Jessie Coulter arrived, ten minutes late and wearing an ill-fitting and wrinkled suit in a shade of blue that was just that much too bright for serious menswear. I tried not to be a snob about his fashion statement, but his tardiness was truly irritating. He was also limping.

"Here, let me get that for you," I said, jumping up to hold back his chair for him instead of letting him struggle with it.

"Thank you," he said, resting his hand on my elbow to keep his balance while he slid into his seat.

"Should, maybe, you be using a cane?" I asked him, not without kindness.

"This? Oh," he huffed at me and waved his hand as if he were dispelling smoke, "old football injury. Flares up from time to time, that's all. No big deal."

"Aha. What position did you play?"

The waiter had just flicked Jessie's napkin into his lap. "Whadda, what?" Jessie asked as the waiter came around the table to flick my napkin. "Oh," he laughed, "you got me! I was the team's student manager and I tripped coming down some stadium steps. So, you see? It really is an old football injury!"

"Ho, ho," I laughed back at him. "So, make your case."

"Jeez," Jessie continued to laugh, "a guy can't even get a drink before he starts talking?"

I motioned to the waiter. "What are you having?"

"What are you having?" he asked.

"Water."

"Oh." He seemed disappointed. "Water for me, too," he said to the waiter.

"Glad that's settled," I told him as the waiter poured. "Now, tell me why you're better equipped to handle Elmer Collier's care, and the disposition of his grandson's estate, than I am."

Jessie took a sip from his now-full tumbler, but made no move to pick up a fork and try any of the food I'd ordered, now arrayed on the table. "Because I'm here, primarily. Meaning, the primary reason I'll be able to do a better job is that I'll be here, in town, so I can do oversight from a more local, you know, location. And I could be there at a moment's notice for any emergency."

"So"—I toyed with a piece of shrimp at the end of my fork—"Elmer starts to breath funny in the middle of the night, you're going to get the call and get out of bed and go over there to—where was it you dumped him? Sunset Gardens—"

"A very nice facility—"

"You're going to go over to Sunset Gardens and sit with him, supervise his nursing care until he's better?"

"Well, that's not usually what I'm called upon-"

"Yeah, me, either. Because that's not *primarily* why Elmer needs a good guardian. He needs a good guardian so some bottom feeder doesn't come along and move him out of his home and into a shithole just so the said bottom feeder can make a few bucks."

That made Jessie sit up. He took another sip of his water, and dabbed the corners of his mouth with his napkin before he replied. "I am an expert at the disposition of estates in the state of Florida. If the idea of having an expert on Elmer's side doesn't move you to see the wisdom in having me on board, then maybe what we need to talk about is how *inexpert* at these matters you are."

"What the fuck are you talking about?"

"Well, for example, you're apparently unaware that your first obligation is to see to it that the estate doesn't run out of money while the principle is still among the living. It's an awful waste of money to have him at Sunshire—"

I started to interject, but Jessie simply talked louder.

"—but even more to the point, you have already proven that you're not being responsible with Elmer's money—"

"I most certainly am not—"

Jessie raised his voice another decibel. "—you spent over fifty thousand, as far as I can tell, on a party at Club Boi—"

"On Eddie's memorial party, and not a huge lay-out when you consider the size of the estate—"

"—where, as far as I've been able to discern, over thirty thousand dollars was raised in support of a local charity which, unfortunately, when I checked with that charity this morning, had received none of the funds and, further, were unaware that any funds were supposed to be forthcoming—"

"That's just because I haven't had the time to donate it yet—I'm even going to match the dona-tion, dollar-for-dollar, you know, so I certainly had no plans to *steal* that money, for crying out loud, if that's what you're implying—"

"—and, what this all makes me wonder, is how you plan to profit from being Elmer's guardian—"

"I don't plan to profit—"

"—I mean, aside from the management fees that would be due to you, and pocketing charita-ble donations, do you own a stake in Club Boi, by chance?"

I shut up before Jessie raised his volume to the level that everyone in the restaurant would be turning to look at us, and not only the select few seated at tables nearby.

"I think," Jessie said, "that the thing to do, Clint, would be to petition the court for your bank records, let a judge look them over, see if he finds anything that might lead him to question the reasons for your interest in the Elmer Collier matter ..."

I wasn't sure I believed that Jessie Coulter would actually do that. Or that he could even get a judge to issue an order forcing me to open my banking records to him. But the threat, the mere making of it, propelled me to my feet and out of the restaurant. I was sure I could have taken the slimy little fuck, but I was also positive that beating the shit out of an opposing party wouldn't improve my position in the court.

I was to regret for decades, however, that I didn't pick up the dish of ceviche and dump it down the front of his cheap blue suit.

Chapter 40

Jack and Avril, his secretary, were behind closed doors having a cigarette when I walked in his office. The air was so thick with smoke I had to use my hands to fan it away before I could see them clearly. This obviously wasn't the only cigarette either of them had had during this smoke break.

"You're killing yourselves and anyone else who walks through this door." I coughed.

"You are a whiner, Clint. Does that ever get tiring? Whining all the time?"

"Remember those envelopes I handed you at Eddie's party?"

"Sure."

"What did you do with them?"

"Put them in my car, like you told me to. They didn't all fit in the glove compartment, so some of them are under the passenger seat."

"I need them."

"Right now?"

"Yesterday."

"Would you mind?" Jack fished his keys out of his pocket and held them toward Avril.

"My pleasure, boss," she said, stubbing out her cigarette, pocketing the keys and making her way to the building's parking garage.

"You want to tell me why your ass is on fire?" Jack asked me after she'd gone.

"Yeah, sure. That lawyer that was assigned to take over for Elmer Collier?"

Jack shrugged.

"He just accused me of trying to pocket Eddie's memorial money."

"Well, that's ridiculous, of course—"

"Of course it is. But the truth of the matter is that I was so hung over I forgot the AIDs Project money. Just didn't even think about it until that schmuck reminded me over lunch, and now he thinks he's got something over on me—"

"You've had a lot on your plate these last few days."

It was as viable an excuse as any, and still I demurred. "It's not like me to forget about a sum of money like that."

"I don't think it's early-onset Alzheimer's," Jack said. "Not yet."

"Don't joke, Jack." Elmer's pale, slack face flashed before me. "Don't joke about that."

"Mr. Test-y," Jack offered in reply.

He was my best friend, wasn't he? He needed to be more invested in my dilemma. "Also, the schmuck told me he'd have my bank records subpoenaed if I fight him for guardianship."

That got his attention. His next move was to immediately hit his phone, dial Xavier and put him on speaker.

"The point is," I said, "yes, it's a threat, but I don't think he'd really go through with it. Xavier, you know how these shit-suckers work—and, Jack, you and I know all about bullies, they make noises about how menacing they are, but they rarely act on them. They're cowards, at heart. They just like to scare the shit out of you."

"The point is," Xavier weighed in, "what's incriminating in your banking records? Let him have them if that's what he wants, all they'll do is prove that you have no need to steal from the Collier fellow."

Then Jack jumped in with his own, exasperated point: "Don't you two see how vulnerable that would make Clint? Why would you even take that chance? Opening up any of your financial records to a charlatan? You never know how those people are going to interpret what they find out about you, or how they'll twist it to use against you. You threw Eddie exactly the kind of going-away party he would have wanted and the creep's already trying to use that against you. What do you think he'll do when he finds out Eddie's your former employee? From when you ran an escort service? And that you spent time in jail when that service was busted? If you're serious about wanting custody of the old guy, Clint, you've got to find a way around Jessie Coulter digging into what you're all about."

My brain actually hurt.

"How is that little shit Jessie Coulter even involved?" I wailed. "There is no part in any of this where he's needed, except that now, just because the judge, or his secretary, or whoever, fucked up some paperwork, now he has the upper hand? How did this become a matter of me proving to Jessie fucking Coulter I can handle taking care of one old man and, importantly—critically importantly, here—why is it the old man is the one who has to suffer in some shitty nursing home while we figure this out?"

I shouted my piece, and the room was quiet.

"Clint," Xavier said.

"No, Xavier," I replied, "I can assure you this is not just a matter of me wanting my own way and wanting it now."

"That's not what I was going to say. I was going to ask you if you'd had the opportunity to go by Sunset Gardens and take a look around."

"I have not."

"So, then, that's something you might want to do," Xavier said. "Think about it, Clint," he said before I could jump in and object, "who told you Sunset Gardens isn't a desireable facility? Donna McAdam, right? You're taking the word of a business rival that the place is a dump. Maybe it's not."

It was an angle I hadn't thought of.

"Just go and see for yourself before we start asserting your rights to Elmer Collier, and taking whatever heat Jessie Coulter will throw your way because of it. Just go have a look."

I drove, first, to my condo to pick up my check book, and then to Lucy's Diner, a small, family place which Jorge Estrella, the current Chair of the Miami AIDS Project, had suggested would be a good halfway point for us to meet. The organization was new on the scene, founded just the year before, but I'd known about it even before Eddie had named it as the beneficiary of his estate. I was already aware of the good work it did for communities impacted by HIV/AIDs and substance-abuse diseases. I was happy to meet Jorge, a short, dark man with intense blue eyes, and hand over the envelopes from Eddie's memorial.

He and I sat in the diner, over some inexplicably good coffee, opening the envelopes, jotting down the names and addresses of the donors—so Jorge could make sure they received the appropriate tax documents for their donations and I could send them thank you notes—and counting up the tally.

"Forty-four thousand dollars—and change." Jorge seemed amazed at the amount and I, too, was pleasantly surprised at the generosity of Eddie's friends and fans. I was happy to write Jorge a check to match the total amount.

"This is going to go a long way," Jorge told me. "I don't think we've ever had so many funds available at one time." He grinned. "Or, no, let me correct that, I *know* we haven't."

I smiled, but I didn't say a word to him about the Miami AIDs Project being the beneficiary of Eddie's—and, hence, Elmer's—entire estate. I didn't know this guy, and I didn't want him to get any ideas in his head, thinking he might have a right to know how Eddie's—now Elmer's—money was being spent while Elmer was still alive.

What I did say was that I hoped he'd find an appropriate way to acknowledge Eddie's name as the funds were being used. "You know," I said, "you could use the money to host a Five-K Run as a fundraiser, call it the Eddie Collier Five-K Run, something like that. He was well loved, so I have to imagine his name will also be a draw. I might even fly in and run it myself."

Jorge nodded, smiling back at me. "I think we can manage that."

Chapter 41

Next I drove to Homestead, the area of Miami in which the much-maligned but not-yet-experienced Sunset Gardens was located. Xavier's pep talk—maybe Sunset Gardens was a garden of paradise?—gave me shallow yet real hope that I would not have to enter into legal battle with Jessie Coulter. Perhaps Elmer Collier was in fine hands at his new home and I could put the responsibilities Eddie had left to me behind me with a clear conscience. If Sunset Gardens really wasn't a shithole, as Donna McAdam had claimed, all I would have to do was swallow hard and choke down Jessie's threat as I struggled to speak the words that I wouldn't challenge his custodianship.

My thin hope began to dissipate before I'd even pulled into the Sunset Gardens parking lot, because I could not, at first pass, even find the parking lot. My GPS led me on a goose chase through a residential neighborhood, instructing me to take what seemed to be an endless series of right-hand turns, until I realized that what it wanted me to do was to turn into what looked like a driveway between a yellow wood-paneled 1950s ranch and a fairly recently whitewashed faux-stone McMansion.

The driveway was long, perhaps an eighth of a mile, and opened to a small, irregular paved lot —six or seven lined spaces reserved for employees, all but two of them filled, and a measly three spaces allotted for visitors and located beside a giant green dumpster. There was a walkway that led from the parking lot to what appeared to be the rear exit of a former elementary school—one sprawling story, built of the sort of pale-yellow brick that had been a popular material for public buildings in the 1970s, drooping gutters over the wide windows that lined the back side of each of two wings, and missing asphalt shingles on the roof belying the building's age.

I stepped up to the walkway, sure the door I was headed toward was an exit—it was large and metal and without any visible hardware that might have allowed me to pull it open. I looked for a bell to ring and, finding none, knocked.

I heard voices behind the metal door, as if I'd startled several people who'd been standing on the other side of it, and the door creaked open. A janitor, from the looks of his uniform, had pushed the long metal panic bar inside the door to admit me, though the two women who were standing with him seemed less inclined to allow me to enter. The disagreement, conducted exclusively in Spanish, a language in which I am less fluent than might be suspected after my long sojourn in Mérida, was heated. All three of them had paper cups of coffee in hand, and one of the women was smoking a cigarette that she used to gesture at me, her arm moving in wide circles, her admonishment clear in any language, "Go around to the front."

But where was the front? How did one get there? The path I'd taken to this metal door was the only walkway I could see.

"It is confusing," the janitor offered, in English. "You have to go back up to the top of the parking lot and there is a sidewalk there. But"—he smiled at me and waved me inside—"you are here now, so you come with me."

Under the disapproving glare of his two companions, the janitor led me into, and quickly through, what was clearly a combination break room and storage closet, containing a square, folding card table with three of its four matching chairs set up between a mop sink, currently occupied by one mop still dripping and filthy—waiting, perhaps, for a rinse when break time was over—and a wall of floor-to-ceiling shelves that held a variety of cleaning chemicals in enormous, plastic, bulk-buy bottles.

"You go out here," he said and ushered me out a door at the other side, into a fan-shaped sort of reception area.

The sounds hit me first, of course—the long, low wailing, the grunts and groans mixed in with the shouted and sometimes coherent demands: "I told you I wanted two Jellos!" and "I am waiting here naked for a sponge bath!" and "I have to pee!"

Then there was the smell. The tang of un-
washed armpits and unemptied bedpans, the
urine fighting a battle with the disinfectant for
primacy. The reception area was too bright, blinding sunshine streaming in an entire curved wall
of windows, and I walked with squinted eyes toward what appeared to be the information desk,
wondering if Pedro would ever be able to remove
the stink of overcooked vegetables, dirty feet, and
farts from the light sport coat I was wearing.

My eyes had better adjusted to the glare by the
time I reached the desk, where no one waited to
greet me or any other visitor. I looked around
for help, at the people all around me—old people crossing laboriously one wing to the other with
the aid of their walkers, old people strapped into
wheelchairs parked just outside their rooms in either of the long hallways that stretched from reception, all of them in hospital gowns and wearing vacant, overmedicated stares. I wondered if
the ones who were moaning were doing so only
because the staff was still waiting for *their* meds
to kick in.

Although I couldn't have verified that immediately with an actual staff person because there
was not one of them anywhere I looked. There
was, however, a bell on the reception desk that
you could push with your palm to summon help,
and I debated pounding on it as hard as I could
until staff came rushing from all directions to see
to my needs. Fortunately I thought better of that
plan—*No need to let the terrible frustration of the
last several days turn you into a complete asshole,*

I told myself. I opted instead to stand by the reception desk and time how long it was going to take for a staff member to appear and notice my presence.

It turned out that the important part of my secret dare was the latter piece: I saw three young people, all who passed my test as employees, not residents, pass through reception before twenty minutes had expired and a fourth finally turned her head to me and stopped. "Can I help you?"

I could have assumed she was a nurse's aide, or an orderly, from the way she was dressed, but it seemed, except for the janitor I'd met on first arrival, all the younger people in the place were wearing the same costume of limp scrubs and tennis shoes. I therefore addressed her neutrally: "Yes, thank you. I'm Clint Kennedy and I'd like to visit your patient Mr. Elmer Collier."

"I don't know any Collier," was her reply.

Instead of allowing myself to meltdown, as I desperately wanted to, I said, "Well, he's a newer patient, so maybe you haven't met him yet. Will you please find me someone who might know Mr. Collier?"

"Sure," she told me.

I waited another ten minutes for someone else to find me in reception, this time another woman in scrubs, but this one older and evidently more familiar with the layout at Sunset Gardens or why would she have agreed to show me to Elmer's room?

"Who you looking for?" the second woman asked me by way of greeting.

"Elmer Collier."

"Huh," she grunted, adding to the other random sounds of discomfort. "I don't know, but follow me … we'll look for him."

Whereupon the older woman proceeded down the left hallway, gesturing for me to follow her, mumbling audibly, "Collier," and "No, not here," as she checked the charts in plastic bins on each door to patient rooms. "Yeah," he must be in the other wing," she said when we'd reached the end of the left hallway and went striding back the way we'd come and into the other side of the building, me following in her wake.

"Here you go! Collier!" she said triumphantly, standing aside for me to enter into the third room we'd come to in the second hallway. Then she disappeared before I could say so much as "thank you."

Elmer had a roommate, a woman shrunken down into the pillows of her hospital bed, a remote control gripped in bony fingers, flicking among channels. I offered her a nod and a "hello" as I passed by to the far side of the room—Elmer's side—but she didn't return my greeting and I felt no reluctance about snapping closed the white curtain between the beds, so Elmer and I would have some privacy.

Elmer lay, unconscious, oblivious, seemingly content, in his bed. Could he tell that the room he was in had peeling puke-gray-green on its walls. Could he hear the discomfort and misery of his fellow patients? Could he smell the odor all around him, feel it, as I did, seeping into his pores.

"Hey, Elmer." I stood over his bed and greeted him.

Was he able to sense that the care he was receiving was of such a different caliber than that he'd been used to just a few days before? Could he tell that he was no longer the recipient of the sort of love and attention that had been heaped on him at Sunshire? Could he feel that he was no longer in a place where he paid enough for love to be included in the monthly fees?

"Elmer, listen, I'm sorry. I'm working on getting you out of here. I promise you. I'm working on it."

I exited Sunset Gardens and walked around the long concrete block path back to the parking lot and my car. When I was seated, I turned the car over and got the air conditioner running before I dialed Xavier.

"You know how you thought a visit to Sunset Gardens might help to allay any guilt about turning Elmer's care over to that Coulter fellow?"

"Yes?"

"Yeah, it didn't help at all."

Chapter 42

"You want to take me to dinner?"

"I do!" Laine insisted. "C'mon. It's the least I can do for my lonely new friend."

She was joking, but her call was more than welcome—it was uplifting. I had driven home from Sunset Gardens and immediately jumped into the shower and, now, though I was freshly washed and dressed in clean clothing, the smell of the place had embedded itself as if in my very nasal hairs. It was a depressing smell, a stink that was getting all over my bad mood and making it worse.

"All right. Where do you want to go?"

She told me to meet her at 109 Burger Joint in half an hour.

There are burger joints and there are burger joints, and then there is the 109 Burger Joint. I opted for the classic—an all-American cheeseburger. Laine went for the Mac Addict—a regular burger topped with mac and cheese—and a side of truffle fries.

"Do you eat like this all the time?" I asked the doctor.

She rolled her eyes at me. "Do I look like I eat like this all the time?" she asked in return, and added a chocolate shake to her order.

"You know, I really did just call you up because I like your company... and because I needed an excuse to come here for dinner, you know? You can't just go to a burger joint by yourself. That would be just pathetic." Laine laughed. "But, now that you're here, I have to say, you look like shit.

I laughed, and shrugged, acknowledging that she was no doubt entirely right.

"So, what's been eating you, Gilbert Grape?" she asked, and took such a large bite of her burger I had no choice but to either start talking or leave us sitting in silence.

"Elmer."

"Is he all right?"

I sighed and shook my head. "There was, apparently, a clerical error, on the part of the court. He was assigned a public guardian and got moved out of Sunshire before I knew what happened."

"To?" Laine went for a truffle fry.

"To Sunset Gardens."

At the mention of the facility, Laine gasped, inhaling the fry so she had to cough to clear her throat.

"I know," I said, reaching over to pat her on the back. "I've seen the place myself—I wouldn't subject Abe Cohen to spending his last days in that pit."

"Who's Abe Cohen?"

I sighed again. "Just someone I know... and don't like very much."

Laine smiled. "So, you straighten out the error and get him back where he belongs, right?"

I nodded. "I wish it were that simple. The lawyer who got the assignment wants to fight me on it." I tried laughing, to see if it would make the situation seem less dire, but it didn't. "He's accusing me of being in it for the money."

Laine sat back in her chair. "Well, we know that's just not true—"

"Right? Not to mention that even if I were, that's the pot calling the kettle black because you can be sure *he's* not in it for any other reason."

"So what are you going to do?"

"What can I do? I've been to Sunset Gardens. I have to see this through. Somehow."

Laine smiled again; I'd provided the only answer she would have accepted. "I'll testify for you."

"You'd do that? I mean, if it comes to that?"

"Of course I would. That's what friends do for each other, dude."

I supposed, as I waved at Laine and watched her drive out of 109 Burger Joint's parking lot in her frog-green Prius, that if she knew more about my life, my past and/or my present line of work, she might feel less generous toward me. Or maybe not; she had such an open, big-hearted spirit she might pick up so much of my baggage and carry on without breaking her stride. I knew only that I would never be a very good friend for her, the same kind she was being for me, because I'd always have too much to keep from her. I'd never know how she'd judge me because I'd never tell her what I really did.

This was as far as I got in ruminating about the puzzle of Laine, however, because my cell started to ring. I glanced down at where it lay on the console of my car, and saw that it was Pablo calling.

"Hi," I said when I answered.

"Clint! I am very glad to reach you! I wanted to let you know that I am looking forward to your homecoming—shall we have dinner tomorrow evening, at my home? I'll have Berta make the fish stew you like so much—"

It was out of the blue, and it was all I'd wanted to hear for a week, and now I had to say, "I can't."

"You have other plans tomorrow evening?" Pablo asked.

"No, it isn't that. I have a... I have a problem here that I have to fix before I can leave."

"And this problem is?"

"Nothing to do with the bank," I assured him quickly. "It's just, a friend of mine died..."

"I am sorry to hear this."

"Thank you, Pablo, but it's his grandfather that's the problem. I agreed—years ago this was —but I agreed to be his grandfather's guardian, if something ever happened to my friend."

"This is very Christian of you. What is this man's name?"

"Well, sure. It's Elmer Collier. He's got dementia, basically is in a coma as a result, and now, I'm his guardian, or I should be, but there was a mix up as we moved his case through the court. The court-appointed attorney, fellow named Jessie Coulter, is, well, I guess he's fighting me for custody of the old guy."

"And we know why he would do this?"

"Sure we do. Elmer's got a nice, fat estate, and Coulter wants a piece of it."

When Pablo replied, what he asked was, "This Coulter. Is he beloved?"

I burst out laughing. "No, Pablo. No, he is not. He's moved old Elmer into what is essentially a warehouse for the elderly, and I can't leave Florida until I get this mess straightened out and Elmer back into a decent nursing home."

"All right," Pablo said slowly. "But don't take too long, Clint. You've been away a long time, and I would like you to be home."

"I would like that, too," I assured him.

I wanted to go back to Mexico more than I wanted most any other thing—I wanted to be in my own home, to read the papers with my feet hanging in the shallow end of my pool, to jump into that pool to cool off before getting dressed to go to my friend Pablo's house for a delicious dinner. To be reassured that Pablo was safe, that *I* was safe, and that our business was intact after the recent housecleaning. To have all the information I needed in order to assess my next move.

Which was possibly moving myself out of the money-laundering trade.

Pablo and I hung up and I didn't hesitate a moment to punch in Jessie Coulter's number.

"Jessie Coulter, Law Offices," a secretary answered.

"May I please speak with Mr. Coulter. Tell him it's Clint Kennedy."

Jessie picked up almost as immediately as his secretary had put me on hold. "Mr. Kennedy."

"Hi, Jessie. Look, here's the thing, we're both reasonable men, right? Let's try this one more time. You have some time tomorrow we could sit down and talk through Elmer Collier's best interests?"

It took Jessie a few seconds more to get back to me this time, and when he did he said, "I have a completely full day tomorrow, you know? You're as busy as I am, you don't get Saturdays off either."

"Oh, I'm busy, Jessie," I said to him. "You're not going over my head. What about tomorrow evening, then? It's Halloween, and I have a party I have to go to earlier in the evening, so, say, around nine?"

"Nope, nope, running until at least ten," Jessie replied.

"Then ten it is," I agreed. "I'll come to your office," I added, and hung up before he could tell me no.

Chapter 43

Saturday, October 31, 2009

DURING my childhood, I had experienced every Halloween I actually remembered at the Cohens'. I'd been a pirate, a zombie, a blob of green goo, and, once, the green Mighty Morphin Power Ranger to Jack's blue. No matter what costumes we'd decide upon, Candace made a fuss about the holiday—as she made a fuss for every holiday—stringing orange lights up at the front of the house and among her climbing roses, carving jack o'lanterns and arranging them with candles all up and down the front steps, hiding speakers in the shrubbery around the front door and putting a tape filled with scary noises—shrieks and evil, cackling laughter—on the stereo to give every kid looking for a candy hand-out a real chill.

As kids, we'd eaten lady fingers that looked like actual mutilated fingers, with cherry preserves for blood; and "dirt cupcakes" with gummy worms crawling in chocolate mud; and eyeball lollipops, and brain taffy and green, "poisoned" candy apples.

This year, Candace managed to put out a spread of sugar that topped even my most joyous Halloween memories. Abe's kids were going to get nothing less than what we had enjoyed as boys, though Candace, considering Abe's recent ordeal, had left the lady fingers off the menu. There were two silver punch bowls on a large buffet in the dining room, one with regular mulled cider for the kids, and one with spiked mulled cider for the grown-ups. I ladled from the grown-up bowl, a cup for Jack, and one for me, and when David asked for a refill, Candace didn't object to my filling it from the same source.

"He has to have *some* fun," she reasoned.

Abe's kids, in the Harry Potter and Hermione Granger costumes Candace had whipped together for them, followed in the tradition their father and Jack and I had established as boys: eating far more of the goodies than we wrapped in cellophane and layered on trays to be given out to the neighborhood kids who'd stop by for treats, but by early evening there was a good supply of goodies stacked by the front door, and the kids themselves were all sugared up and ready to head out to see what people in other houses had to hand out to them.

David and Candace had always gone out Halloweening with us, walked us from house to house and stood on the sidewalks as we approached stranger's doors, less to make sure that we remained unharmed by those strangers—the Cohens' neighborhood had always enjoyed the service of a private security force—than to make sure we said "thank you" at each stop. This year, David wasn't in shape to chaperone the event, and Candace preferred to stay back at the house with him so, although the nanny offered, Jack and I stepped up to walk with the trick-or-treaters.

"I don't remember this," I said to Jack as the lady of the first house we stopped at came down her front steps to meet us with a tray of two tiny glasses, each one flaming.

"Adults deserve a treat, too," she said to us. "Cognac with Chambord. It's called a Paris Burning."

"Quite appropriate for this evening," Jack assured her, blowing out his glass and drinking.

We were served small, mad-scientist-shaped beakers of lager two houses down, and wee cans of Coppola sparkling wine at the one across the street. "I don't remember alcohol for the adults being part of the tradition when we were kids, but I can get behind the addition," Jack enthused.

We walked our two little, stunningly well-behaved wizards all through the neighborhood, until the pillowcases they carried with them were filled with sugar. And then Jack checked his watch —nine o'clock was the witching hour, when the holiday was officially over by proclamation of the Homeowner's Association. They made some half-hearted objections to returning to the indoors— there really is something magical about darkness falling on Halloween and I couldn't be too annoyed that they were making a bit of a fuss and, in any case, they were easily distracted by the next activity we promised: the best part of Halloween —going home and crawling into bed and taking inventory of all the goodies in their pillowcases. They let us steer them back to their grandparents' house and then hightailed it up stairs and under the covers to take stock.

"Please, please, don't forget to brush your teeth," Candace called after them. To us she said, "In the mood for a night cap?"

"Whew," Jack huffed and grinned and checked his watch again, "I'd love to, Mom, but apparently it's now a thing to ply the grown-ups along the trick-or-treat route with cocktails. I've had plenty and, anyway, I made plans—"

His mother jumped. "Date number three?" she asked.

She was as stunned into silence as I was when Jack said, "Yes."

"Well then, how about you, Clint?" she asked as she kissed Jack on both cheeks and sent him on his way. "Will you stay and have something with David and me? I'll break out the single malt —that'll be such a treat for David."

"Indeed!" David chimed in, inspired, speech clear as a bell.

I checked my own watch. Nine-sixteen. I had nearly forty-five minutes before I was due to meet Jessie Coulter. I didn't want to be too early, and I didn't want to spend half an hour driving nervously around Miami, getting myself worked up into a state, getting furious all over again that Elmer was still stuck in Sunset Gardens thanks to the maggot lawyer. I was going to have to play

nice with Jessie Coulter if I wanted a quick reso-
lution to my problem, and a shot of single malt, I
decided, would make me nicer.

"I'd love that, Candace."

"Let's go get cozy in the kitchen, then," she said,
fanning her manicured hand at me before bending
to unlock David's wheelchair and whisk him to the
back of the house. "At least one of our boys has
the decency to have a drink with us when we ask
him to." She laughed in high spirits, no doubt due
to Jack's third date.

"Indeed!" David cried again.

I smiled. He must be working hard on rehab
with his nurse. His affirmatives were coming
along nicely. We should all be so lucky, I thought,
to have someone like Candace running interference for us. She made sure that David's focus
was all on getting himself well, unimpeded by
knowledge of a damned thing that might distract
him.

Chapter 44

Miami, Florida, is a city filled with fine restaurants. Nearly every culture in the world is represented among the cosmopolitan culinary choices. Armenian to Jamaican, Pakistani to Swiss, British pub fare to wine bar tidbits—have a craving and fulfill it within one or another of Miami's myriad gastronomic treasures. The international nature of its dining options befit a city that is not only the hub for some of the world's largest cruise ships but home to the largest concentration of international banks in the US.

Jack Cohen and his date, a women's wear designer named Rudy Marsencavitch, opted for seafood. High-end seafood, though, Jack thought, this being the third date and all. Places like Truluck's Restaurant would start to become special-occasion haunts, and he and Rudy would shortly settle into a routine of ordering in pizza and cooking at home.

Jack amazed himself: he wanted to settle into a routine like that.

With Rudy.

With Rudy, the idea of having a boyfriend—a steady boyfriend—no longer totally freaked him out. Even his mother's not-so-subtle hints that she was in the market for an ever-expanding stable of grandchildren no longer pissed him off. He no longer felt the need for that exercise that had doomed so many relationships in the past: the obsessive breaking down of everything that was wrong with a guy until he had no choice but to jettison him. With Rudy—who was not, of course, a perfect human being—the imperfections seemed either inconsequential or endearing, easily dismissed in favor of those things that were right: the quality of his voice, smooth and deep and slow as molasses, befitting the Southern boy Rudy was, notes that struck Jack right in the solar plexus like beams of light, the promises of high energy and happiness, not to mention great sex; the movement of his broad, square hands and his fingers, calloused from all the intricate handwork he put into the garments he created, always purposeful and efficient, his touch a bewilderingly attractive combination of tender and matter-of-fact; the almost imperceptibly crooked front tooth in the middle of the smile that was so big and so real it could blind a guy.

"How did it go at the shop today?"

Rudy had a loft on Brickell Avenue, not far from Truluck's, that was both his workshop and his retail space. A majority of the work Rudy did, his bread and butter, so to speak, was custom, made-to-order work—cocktail dresses or ball gowns for

Miami's high-end fashionistas—but he did pro-
duce a small collection four times a year and sold
the resulting pants and skirts and jackets and
blouses and tunics and dresses from a tiny but
faultlessly designed shop area to the side of his
cutting and sewing tables, five or six of his tailor's
forms like sentries at the entrance, dressed in
the clothing—the colors and fabrics—Rudy was
dictating for the season.

"I took delivery on a shipment of the most in-
credibly mossy green-charcoal Italian crepe de
chine this afternoon. I don't know what I'm going to do with it yet, but the color's so rich—
there's something in those bolts for spring and I
can't wait to start draping tomorrow morning and
figuring out what it is."

Jack grinned. "My mother is all about neutrals
—with a pop of color. That sounds right up her
alley. I can't believe she isn't a customer of yours
—"

"I know my women"—Rudy shook his head—"if
she was one of my customers, I'd have a dossier
on her at this point."

"I will have to introduce her, then."

Rudy sat back in his chair, ostensibly studying
his menu. "So... that means we're going to do the
whole meet-the-parents thing?"

Jack shrugged, as if importantly occupied with
deciding between the stone crabs and the scallops.
"I thought we would," he said.

In return, Rudy flashed his brilliant smile, and,
but for heroic self-control, nearly knocked Jack
out of his chair.

Rudy—knowing the effect he had on Jack because Jack had exactly the same effect on him—threw him a lifeline, a change of topic to occupy them until Jack's blood pressure dropped back to normal and that lovely pink blush faded from his face. "How did it go at the bank today?"

However Rudy had intended the question, Jack saw it as loaded, the very innocence of it running head-on into what actually happened at the bank every day. Not that Jack let on. He'd very skillfully managed to so far avoid including the nature of his fortune among the revelations he made to Rudy. But that nature was a sticking point that felt, every time he had allowed himself to dwell on it, as if it was a stab to the heart: how the hell would he explain the drug money to Rudy? Should he explain it? What happened ten years and a mortgage and two kids down the road when Rudy found out, if Jack didn't come clean at the outset?

"Hey," Rudy said, deadly smile still flashing, "what do you say, I'll get the scallops and you get the stone crab and we'll share?"

"I say," Jack said, so relieved for the distraction he almost sighed, "that's a magnificent idea."

Jessie Coulter shuffled his McDonald's take-away bag and super-sized Diet Coke into one meaty hand so he could unlock the door to his office with the other. The only thing better than a Mickey D's drive-thru would be, in his humble opinion, a Mickey D's delivery service. He chuckled at the idea as he limped through his front door and let it bang closed behind him.

The state of his knee was genuinely bothering him—it was still appreciably swollen and an awful shade of puke green beneath his khaki pants, and it hurt like hell to put weight on it. But what was he gonna do? A man had to have his dinner and Carla had bugged out of the office early that day, whining as she went: "I'm not leaving early, it's goddamn Saturday night, Jessie. Jesus, I have a life outsida this office, ya know?" The idea that Carla had a life struck him as hysterical, and he'd had a good laugh while she'd waddled out of the building.

Not that there was anything too damned funny about the state in which she'd left his office. Almost a whole week of working on it and there was still shit all over the floor—even in the poor glow of the parking lot light now illuminating the front office he could see piles of files and shards of glass and jellybeans amongst the dust bunnies in the corners. Not that he was fussy about it, but he wondered when was the last time Carla had even tried sweeping up the place. If she was going to slack off about keeping the place swept he was going to have to hire a cleaning lady to come in, maybe just once a week—and whatever that cost it was going to come right out of that lazy broad's paycheck. He thought about calling her at home right that minute and telling her so and it was only the delicious aroma of his Double Quarter Pounder with Cheese and super-sized World Famous Fries that tempered him.

He limped toward his office, groaning with every pound weighing on his shattered knee, stomach rumbling in anticipation of his feast, when a glint of gold near the filing cabinet just to one side of one of Carla's filing cabinets caught his eye. "What the..."

He turned the lighter over in his hand as he hobbled into his office, dumped his McDonald's bag and soda on his desk, and flicked on his desk lamp. The lighter was out of juice, he discovered when he tried to make it flame, but probably a valuable thing he decided, judging from its weight —likely one of Carla's more precious trinkets—and "EK"... Eek, he thought? Who the fuck stamps something like that on a good lighter like this? He stood the lighter up on the base of his desk lamp, right where Carla couldn't miss it the next time she came into his office. He liked the idea of catching her red-handed, make her a little less likely to argue back when he reminded her that part of her job was to keep the office swept up nice. Chuckling softly to himself, he made his painful way behind his desk, plopped in his swivel chair, and lifted his bad leg up so the heel rested on the up-turned waste basket. It was the least he could do to try to get the swelling to go down.

He was settled in and reaching for the paper bag that contained his dinner when he heard the front door creak open. "Ha," he called out, "decided not to wait to tomorrow after all, Carla? You come back to finally start doin' your job? Make me a coffee, while you're at it, will ya?"

Laine Gordon ate at restaurants all the time. She did not know how to cook, not much beyond popping a couple of pieces of bread in a toaster or warming up a frozen chicken pot pie in the toaster oven. She thought, at thirty-two, she ought to have better survival skills than she did, and would have liked to learn to roast a chicken or boil a potato—to attend some of the classes she saw regularly posted on the public boards at Whole Foods —but her schedule didn't allow her that luxury.

The absolute worst part of not knowing how to cook for herself—of being dependent upon restauranteurs for sustenance—was that she so very frequently had to do it alone. Oh, she tried, all right —she tried to be one of those empowered women who were comfortable dining in their own company, sometimes without even a book to distract them. Laine had tried, once, to make it through a meal, in public and alone, without a book to read; even the waiter had been so unsettled by the spectacle she made he'd actually brought her a collection of tourist brochures from the cashier's desk —"Maybe you will like to look through these," he'd offered, laying them down on the table before her.

Laine sighed. Making friends was another luxury for which her schedule had allowed so precious little time in the four years since she'd come to Miami to practice. There was Aletha, of course —she might have lost her mind with loneliness had it not been for Aletha taking her under her wing—and she'd made, she thought, a good start with Clint Kennedy. Something between them had clicked when they'd met—under the most trying of circumstances, and, for Laine, it had been strictly friend-zone clickage; the man lived in Mexico most of the time, for crying out loud, and she was fairly sure women weren't the first thing he saw on his radar when he was looking for more than a friend in any case—but nevertheless promising.

Still, she found herself letting the host at Mina's Mediterraneo lead her to an out-of-the-way table for two and watching him discreetly remove the second place setting after he'd tucked her into her seat.

"A cocktail to start, Madame?"

"Lemon-thyme drop," Laine said. Something refreshing. That wouldn't get in the way of the wine she planned to order later with the osso buco, but that would efficiently and quickly take the edge off.

The waiter walked away and Laine settled back in her seat, resting her pretty chin on a slim hand as she looked over the crowd. It was an attitude she held for a full two minutes, until the first person in the crowd looked back at her, a good-looking, age-appropriate guy who was obviously on a date with the brunette in a blue cocktail dress seated opposite him.

Laine looked away quickly, the blood rising to her cheeks as the word "pathetic" throbbed through her brain, and she dove for the copy of *The Girl Who Played with Fire* she'd tucked into her purse.

"Mr. Sousa," the maître d' greeted Xavier as he strolled into his own restaurant. He knew the menu and the wine list like the back of his hand —he'd had, he'd proudly tell you, some hand in their creation—and, even so, it was still his favorite place to eat in a city filled with good places.

"Table for nine," Xavier said.

"I have the reservation right here," the maître d' replied. "This way, please."

Xavier led his family—his wife and all the kids, plus a few recently-acquired spouses in tow tonight—to his private table at the back of the restaurant. Along the way he greeted fellow diners, local attorneys and others he knew—a nod of the head or an informal salute, he made it a point to never actually approach a diner's table, assuming they wanted their privacy as much as he wanted his. At the table, he pulled out the chair at his own right hand for his wife, and let the maître d' scramble among the two brothers attempting to be gentlemen and hold chairs for both their sisters and their wives.

When everyone had found his place, and cocktails had been served—even to the youngest Sousa, Emily, who had not yet reached her twenty-first birthday—and Xavier had ordered a bottle of white and a bottle of red, to be chilled or decanted now and served with dinner later, Xavier picked up his martini and held it over the table, toward his oldest son and the petite redhead who sat beside him, his wife. "A toast!" he declared, and just loudly enough that every other diner in the restaurant lifted his or her head to look in the direction of the large table at the back of the room. "To my son, Xav, and his beautiful wife, Kristen, and to the wonderful news they've given us tonight!"

There were audible gasps from some corners of the room though Xavier was still speaking softly enough that his words could have been meant for his guests alone—which they weren't. Sometimes privacy had to be damned in favor of good press. What did the good people of Miami expect next from the man who had been named Best Attorney in Miami-Dade County for all but one of the years in the preceding decade? They wanted absolutely nothing. They wanted him to continue to be the pillar they could lean on in times of distress—an expert in his field, ferocious in their defense, and wholly untainted by scandal. What could put a person at a great distance from scandal? Becoming a grandfather!

Xav gestured with his glass toward Kristen, then raised it toward his father. "You know, she even ordered a martini tonight, not to drink, but thinking that would throw you all off the surprise—the first Sousa grand— Wait for it—*daughter* will be here around the last week in January!"

Xav's brothers and sisters cheered and patted him on the back, and his parents kissed each other, as the other diners that night in Xavier's restaurant burst into applause.

"Last one," Candace warned her husband. "You've had far too many cocktails this evening already."

David accepted the tumbler of single malt from her. "But it's a special occasion—Halloween! And, besides, I'm not planning on drinking this straight down, I'm going to sniff it and enjoy the anticipation of drinking it. It's almost more fun, the anticipating." David's brain was working just fine, since his stroke; even if his mouth was not yet as recovered, Candace was able to perfectly translate every word. "Did you get the kids to bed?"

"Not quite. I think my memory underestimated how long it takes to wind down a sugared-up child. Elinda's up there with them—she'll finish knocking the wind out of their sails. I don't remember it being this hard with our boys."

"We were younger then," David reminded her.

"But just as good looking," Candace shot back and twirled herself—albeit very gently—into her husband's lap.

"Is this safe?" David laughed, wrapping an arm around her so she couldn't go anywhere. "In a wheelchair? With my health?"

"Oh, my God, I don't know, but isn't it nice to have some time alone? Just us, in our own home? No company, and no obligation to go anywhere or entertain anyone! I cannot believe how resistant those kids are to their beds—and I thought Clint would never leave, I mean, he stayed for almost an hour after everyone else was gone—"

David nodded. "I noticed that," he said. "I get the feeling that there's something going on with him, something wrong and he doesn't want to talk about it—"

"Oh, my dear"—Candace flung her arms wide —"what could possibly be wrong? You're getting better, God's in his heaven and all's right with the world!" She closed her arms tightly around her husband and planted a kiss on his lips.

"Still," David said when Candace had freed him, "it's nice Clint feels as if he can come to us when he has a problem, even if he doesn't want to talk about it."

And then he kissed her back.

Chapter 45

CANDACE and David were reluctant to see me go, of course. I hadn't spent as much time with them in the previous week as I might have—as I would have on a normal trip to Florida. My to-do list had been longer than it usually was on trips north but, also, once those kids showed up, I had lost my customary desire to use any excuse I could find to swing by their house and check in. Still, even though there was so much I was keeping from them these days—especially David —it had been a pleasure to be in their company. Comforting. Like being home.

I yawned and turned off onto West Okeechobee Road, toward the address I had for Jessie Coulter's office, eased myself into the flow of traffic, the sea of red tail lights cruising to— Where? Home, I'd guess, for most of them, at this hour. Had I known that Jack had made other plans for the end of the evening and was going to skip out early, I would likely have scheduled my meeting with the lawyer to happen earlier as well. I was punishing not only Jessie Coulter but myself by insisting on this late-night face-to-face—not the first time

I'd been disobliged by my own stubbornness and, likely, not the last.

The parking lot in front of the strip mall where Jessie kept his offices was thoroughly pockmarked with potholes, and two of the three lamps meant to illuminate the sorry lot had flickering or completely burned-out bulbs. Seriously, the whole enterprise looked as if it belonged in the middle of a war zone rather than suburban Florida.

There was only one dim light burning in Coulter's offices, a slice of light coming from an inner office, but the door wasn't locked. "Coulter!" I shouted as I walked in. The front office was empty, as I'd expected it to be at that hour of the night, so I shouted again. "Coulter! Answer me! Where the hell are you?"

The office was a disappointing affair, even in the unfair lighting. No matter where you put your eye, it landed on ugly—cheap furniture, the sort of stuff that was never meant to last in the first place, battered now, after so many years of use. And what wasn't ugly was dirty or in disarray—the filthy carpet on the floor, the corners littered with broken glass and... jelly beans? The even filthier doormat which, surprisingly, had the Citizen's National logo emblazoned on it. The secretary's desk with its drawers hanging open and a little kitchen area where cold coffee stood in chipped ceramic cups and the tiny linoleum countertop was dusted with powdered creamer and pastry crumbs.

I followed the light and picked my way toward the back office, stepping over piles of paperwork, an antiquated filing system that someone had clearly lost control over, and called again, "Coulter!"

When no one called back I tried the door to his inner sanctum, which was ajar and pushed open easily.

That's when I discovered the body.

Jessie's body.

I stood inside the door of Jessie's private office, frozen, eyeballing the scene, gagging and thinking, until I heard the theme from the Sopranos.

Jessie's ludicrous ringtone—those familiar, creeping notes, and the most appropriate words. "Woke up this morning and got myself a gun..."

"No. No, no," I said out loud, a dawning sensation creeping over me, cold and powerful like a fucking iceberg bearing down on the very place where I was treading water to save my life. I yanked my cell out of my back pocket and punched in Pablo's number. "What the fuck did you do!" I grunted when he picked up.

"Where are you, Clint?" Pablo asked in reply.

"You know where I am."

I heard Pablo sigh. "I suggest you leave where you are then."

"I... I can't do that..." I looked wildly around the room, at the corpse before me, as if maybe even Jessie could give me better advice. "I"—my voice was a choked whisper—"*I found a dead body.*" A simple fact, when I put it like that, with but one clear directive to follow: "I need to report this, right?"

There was a moment of silence on the other end of the line while Pablo thought about his answer —as if he was actually taking a beat to think over the question I'd asked. "I think you shouldn't do that, Clint."

I felt all hope flee—or, I felt a sensation I would characterize as hope draining out of me like liquid. "But, I had a meeting with him. What if someone knows about that, his secretary maybe knows I was supposed to meet him here tonight? Someone, I don't know who, who could put me, you know, here, when this happened, and—"

I was clearly panicking. Babbling. Pablo cut me off sharply: "Get the hell out of there. Get in your car and go home. Do it now."

I couldn't speak. I couldn't summon the energy to continue even treading water. If I left Jessie Coulter's office without reporting to the police that his dead body was propped up behind his desk — What would that mean? It would make me a criminal.

A thing I was anyway.

Only now I would be the sort of criminal who knew where the bodies were buried. There would no longer be an escape hatch for me. No taking some easy way out and going back to being a citizen of any other order. I would have made a life-long commitment to Pablo, and the cartels. And claimed crime, for all time, as my preferred lifestyle.

"Clint, are you listening to me? I need you to get out of there. *Now.*"

Chapter 46

Sunday, November 1, 2009

I got out of there all right. Tripped all over the stacks of papers on the floor on my way out.

I sped back to my condo, as Pablo had advised, and when I got inside I stood for a good fifteen minutes with my back against the front door, panting. *What's coming next*, I wondered? *Probably the police to arrest me*, I answered myself. I could see no other end to the night's events. Sure, I was a criminal, but I was also a middle-class, late-20th-Century American kid steeped in X-Men comic books and Arnold Schwarzenegger movies: justice always prevailed, and the good guys always won.

I was now, officially, not a good guy.

I knew the long hours of the night ahead were going to be dismal ones, and there was only one fix for it. I headed to my kitchen and downed my first Sol while I stood at the open refrigerator door, and then I reached for a second. I headed to the bar in the living room and used the next beer as a chaser for the Glenlivet I poured into a shot glass.

Eventually I drew the curtains in the bedroom, blocking out the spectacular view of Biscayne Bay just outside the window, and any sense of a world beyond my black-out curtains. The absolute dark was so very soothing; I collapsed into the cocoon, onto the bed, my body ready to give it up, though it took much longer for my brain to be ready for rest. I tossed and groaned in the sheets, waiting for the knock at the door that would penetrate my fuzzy consciousness and force my unwilling body to rise and surrender.

Sleep wasn't entirely elusive, merely not as desireable as the sort of numb-drunk state of wakefulness I'd achieved—I drifted off several times and then woke with a start from a riotously obvious dream: Jessie Coulter sitting up at his desk, a festering hole in between his eyes but otherwise all smiles, waving his intact pinky finger at me. I wouldn't die from lack of sleep; my conscience would kill me first.

Chapter 47

In all the years she'd worked for Jessie Coulter, he'd made some outlandish demands on her, that was for sure. Carla Nicholson had picked her share of locks, taped her share of conversations, fudged her share of reports on his behalf. In their younger days, she'd even posed once or twice as his wife, a masquerade that had them both in stitches. She and Jessie got along with each other because neither of them got along with anyone else. The relationship between boss and secretary could be an intimate one, even more than a marriage, and neither of them had the slightest inclination in that regard. Jessie would have done without a secretary as he did a wife, entirely, if he'd thought he could manage it; Carla, if she were ever to marry, would have, in any case, preferred to take a wife as well.

But this time Jessie had asked almost too much of her, telling her she had to show up for work on a Sunday, all because that crazy woman had thrown a fit in the office over Ethel Nestor and the office still looked as if it had been hit by a hurricane. Sundays were her day of rest—not that she was religious, but a person had to draw the line somewhere when she worked for someone as needy as Jessie Coulter. "Buy me glazed." "Make me a coffee." "Yeah, just write last Monday's date in there when you notarize it."

This time he'd offered her a deal when she'd left the night before: come in on Sunday and get the office so it doesn't still look like shit on Monday morning and I'll slip you an extra fifty, cash, or don't come in on Sunday and then don't bother coming in on Monday either.

Carla was realistic about her life. She had never been very good at managing money, so, even at nearly sixty, retiring wasn't an option. And losing her job wasn't acceptable either as, she understood, getting another job at her age would be a challenge she just didn't have the energy for.

She arrived at the office at around eleven on Sunday morning. She picked her way across the treacherously pocked parking lot, office key in hand, and was surprised to find that the key was unnecessary—the front door was unlocked. "Huh," she said out loud. "Jessie?"

Carla elbowed the door open, wiggling inside with her purse and her neon-orange tote, as well as a small, rolling suitcase she sometimes brought in to collect loot. Those times when Jessie wasn't supposed to be around. "Jessie!" she called, and noticed that his door was ajar, and his desk lamp was lit.

Not that you needed more illumination than the damned overbearing Florida sun to see that the office was a holy mess. She'd worked for days to pile

the files in stacks both alphabetical and chronological—more or less—and right now it looked as
if Jessie had been looking for some document at
the bottom of every other pile on the floor. "Jesus Christ, Jessie, I'm never gonna get this place
cleaned up if you keep making the mess worse!"

She parked her rolling suitcase by the side of her
desk, her purse on top of it, and rolled the neon-
orange tote into itself and stuffed it behind the
lumbar pillow on her desk chair. With Jessie's
injury, she didn't think he was going to come
sauntering out of his office and catching on that
she was planning to take home some booty in all
her empty bags, but why take chances? "How's
the knee?" she called, and noticed that four of
her five desk drawers were standing open—some
more, some less—and her Christmas tree-covered
box of trinkets had been pushed forward in the
bottom left drawer. Exposed. No longer tucked in
as she kept it, behind the first aid kit and other
odds and ends she'd thrown in that drawer. What
the hell had Jessie been looking for in her desk?
And what had he found? She dove for the box,
removed its cover and did a quick visual inventory—what was missing? Was anything missing?
What had Jessie found? How mad was he going
to be? She couldn't think—what the fuck was he
doing in the office today anyway? "Jessie, Jesus
Christ, are you deaf?" she shouted. It was always, according to what she'd learned from the
man himself, better to jump on the offensive whenever you were overcome with the need to defend.
"What the hell?" she demanded as she made her

way to Jessie's office and pushed open the door. "Answer me—

"Oh.

"Oh, oh—"

Carla's first thought was that she wasn't really surprised. Wouldn't you just expect something like this to happen to Jessie Coulter? She thought that, all things considered, being dead was as good an excuse as any for not answering her when she'd called to greet him. And she thought that what she should probably do now was to call the police.

On the other hand—it dawned on her as she waddled back to her own desk, as she reached for the handle of her desk phone—when the police arrived, they were going to turn the office into a crime scene. If she didn't want anyone else pawing through her trinkets, she ought to get them out of the office while she could.

Carla had locked the decoupaged box in the trunk of her 1979 Dodge Omni, stuffed under the in-case-you're-stranded-by-the-side-of-the-road-on-a-cold-night blanket that had lived in that trunk for decades, since before her move south from Wisconsin where such precautions were warranted. She was on her way back into Jessie's office, to call the police, when she realized that she might as well pick up a few of the other things she'd come for—toilet paper, and an extra toner cartridge, and a jar of the powdered creamer and she might as well take the rest of the Keurig cups while she was at it. Jessie wasn't going to be bellowing for a cup any time soon anyway. And the donuts. She looked inside the box from Dough-Rays and was pleased to see there was a cruller left. There were actually quite a few of the donuts left, and they were fairly stale, leading her to believe that Jessie had been dead for a while. Before he could eat them all. And if she didn't take them home with her they would only go to waste at this point.

"Better they go to my waist," Carla said to herself, and laughed at her own joke.

She hesitated over the food on Jessie's desk, however. Much as she loved a good meal from Mickey D's, the soda was probably diluted from the melted ice and flat at this point, and the paper bag was just a little too close to a couple of blood spatters to be appetizing.

She was on her way back to the office from her second trip to the car when another thought occurred to her: What about the money? Had the murder been part of a robbery, or was the money that Jessie usually kept in the locked case in the locked bottom drawer of his desk still there? Money—actual cash—had never been high on Carla's list of things to steal. Maybe a couple of pennies from the take-one-leave-one dish at the cashier's stand, but it was the trinkets—actual things that had been part of the lives of actual people—that had interested her. Still, she knew Jessie kept a great deal of money in that case, and the opportunity was presenting itself—

But wouldn't you know? She went to all that effort—convincing herself to brave proximity to a dead body; overcoming the gag-reaction she had to the smell of the corpse, once she got close to it; oh, so, carefully pushing to one side the upturned waste basket and the leg that rested on top of it so the drawer would clear when she pulled it open—and the drawer was locked.

Carla debated, briefly, having a look around the office or going through Jessie's pockets to get her hands on his keys. But the smell was really starting to get to her.

And it was only money, after all.

And, in any case, once the police got involved, someone was inevitably going to know the money was supposed to be there—some busybody client, or one of the PIs—and taking it might be too obvious. Like, suspicion might fall on her, and she could end up on the wrong side of the person who wanted it more than she did. Because she was the one with opportunity, right? She was one who, after all, found the body.

It came to her: she was going to be the one who found the body! The police, and all the reporters too, were going to want to talk to her, a first-hand eye witness!

The thought cheered her, and she had a little smile on her face as she made her way back to her desk. She picked up her purse and rummaged through it for her hand mirror and a lipstick. She wasn't a vain woman—not a lot to be vain about, she laughed—but she did like a little lipstick.

Carla smacked her lips together, to spread her preferred shade of "All American Rose", and blotted them with a tissue. Then she picked up her desk phone and dialed 9-1-1.

Chapter 48

I'D taken a six-pack of the Sol into the bedroom with me, as well as the bottle of Glenlivet. Each time I woke, rattled from one of the horrifically clichéd dreams to which my psyche was subjecting me, I reached for another shot of something. The beers grew warm as the night progressed, but the knock I was anticipating continued not to come.

I was fully expecting the police. Among the scenarios that were running through my head—and that reliably turned into ever-more disturbing dreams—was one in which Charlotte and Abe, in full police riot-gear get-ups, arrived at my door to take me in, though Charlotte had had to handcuff me because now Abe was missing an entire arm.

But maybe it wouldn't be the police who banged on my door. Maybe an assassin was, even now, sneaking through the rooms leading to where I lay, mere seconds from taking me out too. I still didn't know what was going on in Mexico. Maybe, like Emiliano and Felipe and Matais, I'd made somebody's naughty list?

Probably not Pablo's—though one never knew. Maybe that's why he wanted me home. To take me out on Mexican soil, where I would be most easily disposed of. God knew, cleaning up after my problems with Abe and then with Jessie, I'd given him enough reasons in the last week to think I was a pain in his ass. More trouble than I was worth.

Not to mention, how might David's stroke, and so his current inability to run effective interference for us with the Feds, figure into the calculations of a crime boss? Certainly it decreased my personal value in the equation.

I might well have put myself in the way of a hit. However inadvertently.

I was drunk enough to be comforted by the thought that assassins were generally competent; if one of them was going to take me out, it would probably be painless.

These were the sorts of bedtime musings that might once have had my adrenaline coursing like water through the Grand Coulee Dam. With effort, I tossed once again in my bed and reached my hand to the nightstand for one more warm beer. Tonight it was as if I didn't have a drop of the stuff left to spare.

Chapter 49

THE man crouched behind a parked car, facing the six wide concrete steps that led down to a small incline and into the service entrance of the Miami-Dade Courthouse. It was an easy entrance—all he had to do was time it to when the overnight janitor took his ten PM smoke break out behind the dumpster... and then, wait... Yes, there he was, the security guard, lighting up as he took the incline up, unable to wait for his nicotine fix until he'd joined the janitor.

Inside, the man trod lightly over the cracked concrete floor to the stairwell. The door gave with a slight creak, and he headed upwards. The judge's office was on the third floor; the climb wasn't strenuous. In any case, the man was in good shape. Had to be in his line of work, though in the movies his kind of character was often portrayed as some half-wit slob with a sadistic streak. Had to be fit to be in his line of work, and smart. Though in terms of almost always wearing dark colors, well, the movies got that part right. The better to blend into the night.

It was good luck, the man thought, that the judge was a workaholic. Made his job easier. Much more complicated if he'd had to show up in, say, the man's bedroom to get the job done. In that case he would have had to sneak around the judge's grown sons—who were, as far as the man could tell, true half-wits, or, they must be; they were much too old to still be living at home— and his skinny, brittle bitch of a wife. No wonder the guy worked late, weekends; who'd want to go home to a family of oafs and bitches?

The secretary—Barbara, by name, the man remembered—looked up when he pushed open the door to the judge's office suite. The judge was hard at work, and that broad was going to be hard at work too, he knew—even the most cursory observation of the target would have told a person that Barbara stuck to her boss like toilet paper on the bottom of his shoe. Even at ten o'clock at night. Her sort of dedication was a big, blood-red warning flag to the man—if asked to place a bet, his would have been on something more going on between the judge and the secretary than office work. What kind of a secretary burned the midnight oil like that? What kind would care enough, unless they were banging the guy?

"May I help you?" Barbara asked.

"I'm here to see Judge Kushner," the man said, entering.

Barbara blinked. "Is he expecting you?"

"I don't think so," the man said, gliding past her desk and pushing into the judge's inner sanctum. Barbara stood up out of her chair and sputtered, but she was too disconcerted by the man's mere presence to offer more vigorous objection.

The man closed the door behind him, and the judge looked up as it clicked closed. He had to turn away and spit, quickly, into his brass spittoon before he could stand, and inquire, "What can I do for you?" He forced his voice, so the sound would be even. Not reveal how perturbing the man's intrusion was.

"Yeah," the man said, reaching into the breast pocket of his ink-blue sports jacket. "I found this," he said, withdrawing the judge's Dunhill lighter, and polishing the initials—EK—with his thumb before he set it carefully on the judge's desk blotter. "I thought you might want it back."

"Why..." the judge said. "My... I... I lost this years ago. Where did you find it?" he asked, trying not be marveled.

The man shrugged. "I found it, you know."

The judge allowed himself a smile. "Where?"

"In a dead lawyer's office."

"A dead..." The expression on the judge's face made it clear he was having trouble comprehending the circumstances under which the Dunhill lighter had reappeared; the man shrugged again —it wasn't necessary that the judge have a detailed understanding of how he'd again come into possession of his lighter.

"No worries," the man promised, as if that explained everything, "I just came across it and I wanted to do you a solid by getting it back to you."

"Well," the judge shook his head, still bewildered, "thank you, I guess. Awfully good of you to go to the trouble."

"No trouble, no worries," the man repeated. "But I'm just thinking, now that I've done a solid for you, you'll maybe do a solid for me sometime. How about it?"

Barbara listened carefully, her ear pressed to the door to the judge's inner office. The man who'd barged inside made her nervous, and she couldn't completely make sense of the conversation he was having with the judge, but she was sure there was something juicy going on behind that door. Something she'd be able to use to further her desire to get the judge to leave his wife and retire with her. So far, he'd been able to cover for her work, mistakes she designed to make him seem evermore incompetent and feeble-minded; mistakes not egregious but so consistent he would be forced to vacate the bench as they came to light. The unintended consequence of her success was that the judge now suspected himself of losing his marbles. She hadn't anticipated he'd take a couple of misplaced old people, one or two kids accidentally shoved into foster care, so personally. She wanted him, but with all of his marbles, thank you very much.

But what was this about that stupid lighter he'd lost so many years ago?

What was this about a dead lawyer?

There was definitely something juicy going on in there that she might be able to use…

Chapter 50

Monday, November 2, 2009

I lost a whole day.

A whole fucking day.

I ripped open the curtains at my window, and then backed up, an arm shielding my eyes against the blinding light now slicing into the cool, dark cocoon of my bedroom. I'd never before known what a vampire might feel like, encountering the sun. "Oh, fuck," I grunted as my eyes began to water.

"Sorry to call you so early," Xavier said. It had been his phone call that had awakened me from my self-inflicted stupor. There were empties rolling on the floor by the side of my bed. A bottle of Glenlivet with its lid missing and no more than half an ounce left as dregs sat on my bedside table.

"No, Xavier, it's fine," I said to him, heading toward the bathroom to flush my rancid mouth with some water. "What's up?" I put the phone on mute, turned the faucet on, stuck my head under the faucet and slurped.

"I got a call this morning from Judge Kushner. I mean, the man is known for being efficient, or maybe it's his secretary— But, Clint, that attorney who wanted to fight you over Elmer Collier?"

I choked on the fresh water flowing into my mouth.

"Clint?"

"I'm fine." I grabbed a towel to wipe my mouth. "What about him?"

"He's dead."

I gripped the towel. "Really?" I was trying but, even to me, my voice sounded an octave higher than usual.

"Murdered. Botched robbery is the thinking— and I mean *really* botched. The police found almost ninety thousand in cash locked in a desk drawer. His secretary found him yesterday morning."

"Really?" I repeated, somewhat nearer to my normal register.

"Lucky for you. And I don't know how Kushner got onto it so quickly, but I suppose he heard the news and simply reasoned that, since there was no longer anyone else standing in line to take care of Elmer, it might as well be you."

"Yes," I confirmed. "Lucky for me."

I showered while Xavier faxed the paperwork to Sunset Gardens that would allow me to deliver Elmer back to the cheerful and well-appointed care of Sunshire Elder Care Home, into Donna McAdam's loving if passive-aggressive attentions.

Then I called Tim to check in on the day's transfers, Amelie to tell her to prepare the plane for
an early afternoon departure, and Pedro so he'd
know to make sure the refrigerator was stocked
with Sol and the pool was clean.

All this and I was still at Sunshire by nine AM.
"We're happy to welcome Elmer home," Donna
said, beaming at me as if neither Elmer nor I had
ever left.

I saw Elmer settled back in his old room. Donna
gave the two of us a moment alone. "You take care
of yourself," I said to the man in the coma. "I'll try
to be back in a couple of weeks or so to check on
you." Depending, I thought, on if the police stick
with the burglary story to explain Jessie Coulter's
demise. It pleased me to think that Elmer would
have smiled if he could.

There were quite a few errands I had to run before I could leave Miami. I drove to South Miami, where I'd arranged to meet my real estate
agent to see the inside of the Art Deco shopfront
I was thinking about turning into a branch office. I headed back into downtown Miami so I
could stop by the bank and see Jack—give him
a head's up about my plans for the new branch
and the real estate agent's phone number, so he
could arrange to go see the place himself. I swung
by the Cohens', to say my farewells to Candace
and David, though David was taking a nap when
I got there and I was able to say goodbye only to
Candace—"Don't stay away too long," she admon-
ished me, "because I miss you when you're gone.

Not more than a month, promise me." I promised, and then I headed to my final stop, the Grove, to confirm that the construction crew was back to work on Eddie's houses. I got there later than I had planned, traffic was turning into a bit of a headache due to an accident on Old Cutler Road, but I used my drive time wisely, to make a few calls —to Miguel, who was glad to hear I was coming back to Mexico and updated me on the progress of the new library, and to Darius, who shook my confidence in him by expressing surprise that I'd been gone from Mexico at all, and to Pablo.

"I'm glad you're able to return to your home, Clint. Come to my house for dinner tonight, yes? To my vineyard in Guadalajara. Six o'clock, we'll have drinks among the vines before we eat," he said.

I was in Guadalajara and at Pablo's hacienda in time for cocktails.

There was about an hour of daylight left when I arrived; the vineyard, naked since harvest, looked hazy gold in the setting sun. It was surprisingly cool under the banyan tree, at the edge of a field he'd planted in viognier, where he'd requested a small wooden table and two folding chairs be placed for us. The table was covered with a crisp white cloth, and set with two crystal wine glasses and a silver bucket of ice in which his previous year's bottling of the varietal sat chilling.

The wine, I thought, after Pablo had poured and I had sipped, was unremarkable. I didn't say this to Pablo, of course; I didn't want to insult him, and he knew probably better than I did what an exceptional viognier would taste like. Why rub it in that his wasn't among them? Besides, we had too much else to talk about—Jessie Coulter's death, the Mexican housekeeping, Abe's fucking little finger—to let ourselves be sidetracked by a discussion of winemaking.

Pablo removed his cigar case, a gold lighter, and a small blue cardboard box from the pocket of his white linen jacket and hung the jacket on the back of a chair before he sat down at the table. He gestured me to the other seat. The blue box—an iconic blue Tiffany box, done up with a white satin bow—he sat on the table, and he used his forefinger to push it toward me.

"What's this?"

"For you, my friend. A gift," Pablo replied.

I offered Pablo a puzzled grin.

"Go ahead. Open it."

So I pulled the beautiful blue box toward me, and undid the knot on the satin ribbon. Inside was another box, this time a beautiful black hinged velvet box, the sort that often holds engagement rings, a thought that made me laugh. "What did you do—" I laughed as I opened the box.

Abe's little finger rested—bloodlessly, thank God —inside.

"What is your business?" Pablo asked me before he began what was for him a meditative ritual: trimming his cigar, depositing the stub end in the crystal ashtray his staff had thoughtfully placed on our picnic table, lighting up, closing his eyes to better appreciate the first several, satisfied draws.

"What is my business, Pablo?" I cleared my throat, to try to bring it back down to my normal register, and flipped the lid closed on the velvet box as nonchalantly as I could manage. "I guess I'd have to say laundering drug money," I replied, attempting to put the black box back into the blue box and put the whole, gory gift back on the table, fumbling as if my fingers were no longer receiving signals from my brain.

"No," Pablo corrected me. "Your business is banking. You say 'drug money' but you handle only the money part. I handle the other part, do you understand? From any part of the drug business, any consequences, I can absolve you."

I nodded and took a gulp of the wine, which was not growing on me. "I wish it were that easy, Pablo. But I'm not Catholic."

Pablo laughed. "I think," he said, "that your Jessie Coulter was taking advantage of your friend, Elmer. Would you say that's true?"

"Not *my* Jessie Coulter. Other than that."

"He was using your friend as a way to make money for himself, with no regard for your friend's comfort, or health. And that angered you."

"Correct."

"So, as your friend, I took care of this for you. Is your friend Elmer not better off now?"

I spit out some of the wine, my laughter was so nervous and sudden. "You skipped a few steps putting together the logic of that, wouldn't you say?"

Pablo tilted his head and took a luxurious puff of his cigar. When he exhaled the smoke, he offered two perfect smoke rings in the process. "I'll tell you, Clint, that I have recently had some friends who took advantage of some other friends of mine. I took care of it so all my friends are better off now."

I didn't even know if I wanted to be in the money part of the drug business any longer, but I did want a better answer than that.

Pablo was not, however, in the mood to give me one. Pablo was in the mood to wax philosophical. To opine to the bare, twisted grapevines and the setting sun, and to me, about the integrity of a man who knows his own job and does it well, the corrosive character of unsuitable curiosity and the corrupting power of greed.

And about the nature of trust.

Even had I been willing or unwise enough to press Pablo, I wasn't going to get a straight answer out of him.

Not tonight.

And, you know, Abe's finger was sitting on the table.

So I refilled our wine glasses and stretched back in my chair. Whether or not I was going to remain in the laundry business—whether or not I had the will, or even a *way*, to turn off the money faucet —was a decision that was going to have to wait for another day. Tonight, I was content with the view and the chill that was moving through the slowly falling night air. Content to let Pablo spin his stories, and to reflect on what I myself had learned that day about trust.

When I'd pulled up earlier that day in the Grove, I'd had two goals: nail down a completion date with the crew boss, and find Charlotte.

The first had been easy, though I knew better than to take a contractor at his word; he thought he could have the work done by Thanksgiving and I mentally penciled in mid-February to have Eddie's houses on the market.

The second goal took more doing. I had to go through the flips room-by-room until I located Charlotte, on her knees in a powder room ripping out the linoleum from under a pale yellow, low boy toilet. Fortunately, it was a small room, and she was alone.

"I see you have your job back," I said.

There was no reply she could make, other than to laugh, which, to her credit, she did. "Once I have the linoleum up, I can lift up the toilet and go right after the subfloor. What are you doing here?"

"I need to ask you a question." I squeezed myself into the powder room with her and closed the door behind us before I took her work-gloved hands in mine and lifted her to her feet. "I need to ask if you'll let me be your fallback position."

Charlotte shook her head. "I have no idea what that means."

"It means that after you've gone through all the guys you need to go through before you realize that you and I are supposed to be together, when you realize you have no other choice, you'll swallow your pride and come and find me."

Charlotte sighed. "This all presupposes that I don't hate you."

"It does."

That got a smile out of her.

"And that you'd be willing and able to—"

"To?"

"Drink only white wine for the rest of your life when I'm pretty sure you also like a nice red from time to time."

She looked me in the eye until a rather noncommittal noise came out of my mouth. "Hmmm…"

"Right. Well, even so, just how would we make it work? You live in Mérida and, under the terms of my parole, I'm not allowed to leave the state of Florida."

"I have lots to do in Florida—you have no idea. I'll be here all the time."

"And what would you ever tell the Cohens about me? I know they're family to you, and to them I'm just the chick who sold out their son and put him in prison."

"A bridge to cross when we come to it." I was the dude who got their son's pinky finger chopped off, let's remember. "You have no idea how forgiving the Cohens can be."

"Yeah?" Charlotte shoved at me with her gloved hands. "And what about trust? You know the things I've done"—she narrowed her eyes—"and I know about the things you've done. At least I know some things. How could you ever trust me? How could we ever trust each other?"

This was truly a point to ponder. And it made me smile. "I don't know," I told her. "Honestly, I don't know that I could ever trust you. But I do like that we don't have a whole lot of secrets from each other. I think it's one of the things I like best."

Charlotte look stunned for a moment. And then she laughed again.

I closed my eyes. Pablo's voice droned softly, somewhere in the back of my mind. I wished only that the wine was better.

STAINED FORTUNE, the first book in the Clint Kennedy Series, was rated the #2 Amazon Bestseller, March 2019!

You've just finished **MONEY FAUCET**, the second of Clint Kennedy's adventures.

Now get ready for **HARD CASH**, the third installment of the Clint Kennedy Series coming soon from Joe Calderwood. Sign up for our newsletter and be the first to know when it is released.

mailchi.mp/waterstreetpressbooks.com/ waterstreetcrimemailinglist

Get the Water Street Crime Starter Library
FOR FREE

Get four, full-length ebooks—**BLOODY PARADISE**, **FROM ICE TO ASHES**, **TROPICAL ICE**, and **SING FOR THE DEAD**—plus two introductory short stories by the author of **STAINED FORTUNE** and **MONEY FAUCET** and lots more exclusive content, all for free!

Building a relationship with our readers is the very best thing about publishing.
We occasionally send newsletters with details on new releases, special offers and other bits of news relating to Water Street Press.

And if you sign up to the mailing list we'll send you all this free stuff:

1. A free ebook edition of the exotic thriller **BLOODY PARADISE**—"...a spicy thriller..."

2. A free ebook edition of the crime thriller **FROM ICE TO ASHES**—"designed to shoot the ice down your spine..."

3. A free ebook edition of the eco-thriller **TROPICAL ICE**—"...well-spun, tautly written..."

4. A free ebook edition of the delightfully noir-ish mystery **SING FOR THE DEAD**—Foreword Reviews' Gold Medal winner

5. A free copy of two introductory short stores from the author of **STAINED FORTUNE** and **MONEY FAUCET**—stories from the childhoods of two his most intriguing characters, Alvaro and Pablo.

6. Advance notice about the release of the next novel in the Clint Kennedy Series, **HARD CASH**.

You can get all this and more,
for free, just by signing up at

**mailchi.mp/waterstreetpressbooks.com/
waterstreetcrimemailinglist**

Did you enjoy this book? You can make a big difference for our amazing Water Street Crime authors.

Reviews are the most powerful tools in our arsenal when it comes getting attention for our books. Much as we'd like to, we don't have the financial muscle of a New York publisher. We can't take out full-page ads in the newspaper or put posters on the subway.

(Not yet, anyway).

But we do have something much more powerful and effective than that, and it's something that those publishers would kill to get their hands on.

A committed and loyal bunch of readers.

Honest reviews of our books help bring them to the attention of other readers.

If you've enjoyed this book we would be very grateful if you could spend just five minutes on Amazon or the online vendor of your choice leaving a review (it can be as short as you like).

Thank you very much.

About the Author

Joe Calderwood was born and raised in Homestead, Florida and graduated from college in 1971 with a BBA. For many years he was a practicing CPA in Florida before beginning his career as a serial entrepreneur. He's owned, so far, seven different businesses, currently a fifty-five lot development in Western North Carolina. *Money Faucet* is the second in the Clint Kennedy series. He lives in Western North Carolina with his spouse of six years—though the two have lived together thirty-nine years, only recently the Supreme Court allowed them to marry.

Hard Cash

Enjoy this excerpt from HARD CASH, *the third book in the* Clint Kennedy Series *by* Joe Calderwood.

1

Don't let anyone kid you: crime *does* pay.

At least, that was my take on life in early November 2009.

Pablo and I flew into El Lencero Airport for the funeral on my Gulfstream, not his, because my toy was new and I wanted another opportunity to fly through the skies—even if only from Mérida to Sonora—on my own wings.

He and I wore bespoke suits for the occasion —mine of the most delicate, charcoal-black baby alpaca wool from Hungary, from the hand of the house of Boglioli, and Pablo's of the finest cream-colored Irish linen available to his own Italian tailor, Mr. Massimo Piombo. And we sipped a bottle of Bollinger Les Vieilles Vignes Francaises—from mouth-blown Zalto Denk'Art flutes—as we flew.

Six bodyguards traveled with us—Pablo's, not mine; even given my line of work and all the intrigue it had recently fostered, it had not occurred to me that I might want my own security detail. The men, all in dapper black, shoulder holsters causing not even one errant bulge beneath their sleek-fitting suits, rode at the front of the plane, studiously separated from Pablo and me at the back, yet utterly silent, attuned to the conversation between us and a mere raised finger away from intervening, should— I don't know. Should I suddenly sit up in my seat and raise my voice to their boss? Wag a finger at him? Punch the elegant Pablo in the nose? Even if that was my style, I'm smart enough not to fuck with a bunch of guys who look like they could be extras in a Francis Ford Coppola movie.

"It is not customary to wear white to funerals, in my country," I offered, stretching my shoulders and slouching deeper into the leather of the seat I occupied.

"Nor in mine," Pablo conceded, and then he shrugged. "But what am I to do? I am most comfortable in white linen—it is my signature, you know? If someone does not want me to wear white linen to his funeral, then he should not die."

I chuckled because, really, what else was I supposed to do? Of the dozen—or so—drug lords for whom I laundered money, Pablo Navarro was the emperor, the undisputed leader of the pack. I'd worked for his pack, under his aegis, for just over a year at that point, putting an average of eight million dollars a day through my wringer in Mexico and making it come out all sparkling white and fluff-dried on the other side: in America; the bank I owned in Miami. I took my five percent right off the top and kept my head down, asking no questions and telling no lies. Still, these funerals—all to lay to rest Pablo's fellow lords who'd been taken out in what Pablo described as a "housecleaning", three of them in the course of just five days—gave me pause. I was still unsure what part, if any, Pablo had played in their demise.

I was not looking forward to the funeral, certainly. The first two had been dull, droning affairs involving High Masses and plenty of incense, and I knew what I was in for as we winged our way to Sonora. I had grown up in Southern Florida in the '90s, in many ways a typical American kid, unpracticed in the Protestant faith with which my mother was titularly affiliated, and the rites and rituals of the Catholic lords had intrigued me, at the start; by the third funeral they had lost their mystery. I found the service tedious, the priests long-winded, and the wailing of the widows and other women, shadowed in their black veils, absolutely heartbreaking.

At the first funeral, Emiliano's, in his territory, Mexicali, the week before, I hadn't had the luxury of being bored. I'd just returned to Mexico from a week's enforced vacation in Miami, where Pablo had insisted I lay low while the housecleaning had been in progress, and I was not especially comforted by the idea that Pablo had kept me away for my own good. Sure, he wanted me out of the way while the ranks of his Mexican brethren were being summarily reduced—with or without his direction; again, at this point I hadn't a clue about that—but what was going to happen to me when the housecleaning was complete and I returned to my home in Mérida? Killing me on Mexican soil would be so much more convenient for Pablo, where he had a veritable army of men at his command and the law was disposed to look the other way when he acted out. In spite of the fact that Pablo himself had welcomed me back to Mexico with open arms, I had been on my toes while we laid Emiliano to rest—and only slightly distracted by the intricacies of the Catholic funeral service, watching Pablo to take my cues from him about when to stand, when to sit, when to kneel.

By the time of the second funeral—Felipe's in Matamoros, four days ago—I had moved from a state of constant red alert to a more manageable phase of paranoia: was I still of use to Pablo? I had always understood, on an intellectual level, that the friendship he and I sustained was based on mutual need: he needed me to turn his money into currency he could easily access, and I needed —or, well, at least greatly *desired*—the income I made doing my part of his dirty work. I knew that finding another American banker to take him on as a client would be difficult, though not impossible—it was 2009 when we began our relationship, after all, and a lot of banks, not just mine, were scrambling to stay afloat after the American economic bubble burst. I wondered if Tim, my assistant, had been too efficient about doing the work I delegated to him—running the armored cars to and from Mérida to cartel HQs all over Mexico to collect drug industry profits, and sitting at the elbow of my Mexican banker, Juan Carlos at Reforma Bank, while the day's transfers were processed; perhaps I'd not been hands-on as much as I should have been, delegated thoughtlessly, and now Pablo had come to the conclusion that paying me five percent was wasteful spending. Had he concluded that it would be more profitable for him to simply hire Tim to do the work for a drastically cut rate? I had, however, by the time of Filipe's funeral, some sense that if Pablo wanted me dead and out of the way, it would have happened already. Still, I was in no way comfortable with what the future might hold.

This, the third funeral, the final one, so far as I knew—Matias's in Sonora—found me more willing to relax about my place, and its continuance, in Pablo's organization. I'd been back in Mexico for six full days by this point, and Pablo had invited me for dinner several times—to his vineyard in Guadalajara, to his hacienda near Mérida, and, once, to Kuuk, a favorite restaurant in Mérida where we indulged in the out-of-this-world tasting menu and enough wine that Pablo had dismissed his car and allowed me to drive him (and, of course, two of his bodyguards) back to my place for a nightcap and a dip in my pool. We'd genuinely had a great time together that night; I did not think Pablo was that good of an actor.

Also, I was growing comfortable with my familiarity with the Catholic services. I no longer needed to glance out of the corner of my eye to know when to stand or kneel, and I could sing some of the lyrics, in Spanish, to the more popular funeral hymns. I also knew enough not to try to enter the church immediately upon arrival but to wait outside for the Reception of the Body.

As the congregation recessed from Matias's service at the Catedral de la Ascunsion, the jewel of the forty-nine parishes within the Archdiocese of Hermosillo, Pablo clapped me on the back, commanded, "Come," and steered me away from the steps of the wondrous building, toward where two of his men stood by one of the two shiny, dark-blue Lincoln Town Cars that had been reserved for his use while he was in Sonora. I did so willingly but, as I seated myself, noticed that the driver of our blue Lincoln was not jostling for a place in the funeral procession. He was following the lead Town Car, making a tight left turn away from the cluster of cars at the front of the church, to go in the opposite direction.

This was unusual. After the other funerals we'd gone to the grave sites, then on to the homes of the widows to partake in a feast of outstanding local food and shared memories of the deceased. We'd never stayed at these after-parties, so to speak, for very long, but we put in a showing; that we were clearly going to be skipping this part of the occasion in Sonora put me more closely to the edge than I'd been all week long. Adrenaline poured into my bloodstream as if it came bottled in a gallon jug, glugging into my system in thick, powerful bursts.

Pablo, who'd taken the seat beside me in the back of the car, clamped his hand on my thigh and squeezed just above my knee until it was almost painful. "I've had my fill of grieving," he said, looking ahead, around, at the two men who rode with us or out the windows, but not at me. "I would rather, this afternoon, to have steak." I closed my eyes against the agony Pablo was causing my knee and tried not to wince. "After all, we are in the meat capital of all Mexico!" Pablo might have been thirty years older than I was, but his hands were strong. Like a vise grip on my trembling thigh. "Sonora! Even the word makes you crave beef, no?" he asked and released his hold on my leg.

I managed to take a deep breath, as if sucking in the whole of my thirty-some years on the planet, wondering if I really was going to die so young. Then I felt the hard swat of Pablo's palm on my throbbing thigh. "Yes! Take another deep breath, Clint—you can almost smell the slaughterhouses!"

2

To my great relief, the blue Lincoln took us to Villa de Seris, Restaurant Palominos, and actual beef —two extraordinary, rare *filete supremos*. The cabernet Pablo had ordered to go with our beef was, I noted as he poured, from California—Silver Oak; between us, Pablo was the oenophile, and quite dedicated to growing, bottling, and promoting Mexican wines, so I declined to comment on his choice. Pablo tasted his steak, sipped his wine, declared that both were "*Excelente*!" and, turning to the window we were seated before, gave a little salute to his men who waited outside. "Rafael," he called, gesturing to our waiter with his knife and ordering steaks to be sent to his security detail.

We tucked into our food then and, still fighting the trace adrenaline making my heart beat double time, I let Pablo take the lead in our conversation. Clearly, he had something he wanted to say to me. "Well, now we have buried three of our own..." was how he chose to begin.

I looked at the steak bleeding on my plate. "Not *our* own, I think," I replied. But softly.

Pablo chewed, swallowed, drank, returned his glass to its place on the table, put his fork on his plate, and lifted his napkin from his lap to his lips. Only when he'd wiped away a drop of cabernet from the corner of his mouth did he smile. "I know that you have been wondering what's happening here in Mexico while you were away," he said, "and I think I would like to tell you."

I nodded, grateful that I had a mouthful of steak and couldn't speak.

Pablo lifted his wine again and sat back in his chair. "From time to time, every business must reassess its operations, steer itself back to its core strengths."

I frowned. I was used to Pablo talking in metaphors and euphemisms, but I was not used to him talking like an MBA candidate. I took my time chewing.

"Our departed fellows in these border towns," Pablo continued, waving a hand to indicate geography, "they were not content with the profits they enjoyed from our core business. They wanted to expand their interests, into areas where they have no expertise—and for which we have little taste."

I looked up and caught Pablo's eye. "We?" I asked.

"Me. *I* have little taste for human trafficking, Clint. Our pathways into the US gave these men some notion they would be able to transport people as well as our more customary wares, and I do not like this."

I didn't immediately think adding 'coyote' to the drug runners' job descriptions was a completely unreasonable business decision. I, too, had interests beyond the work I did for Pablo and his cohorts, and none of them got in the way of my taking good care of his business. "If they could help to safely get people to a better life, a life that the people themselves desire, why not?"

Pablo had picked up his utensils again, in preparation to cut another piece of steak, but instead of targeting the beef on his plate he pointed the knife at me. "One hundred thousand pesos at the start! This is what they were asking! *Ladrones*! Before they would even let the people stuff themselves into their boat or their truck or their tunnel, they asked for one hundred thousand pesos, and on the other side, they said to the people, 'Oh, you think you have paid for this trip? No, no!' and demanded one hundred thousand more! If the people or their families did not or could not pay, they held them for ransom. Kept them imprisoned in the hull of a boat or a metal shed on a *bastardo* rancher's land just over the border from this very town. They gave them no food, no water, no relief and, if they died in captivity? Well, this is the cost of doing business! Many innocents died for their greed!"

At this point Pablo put down his knife and shoved a huge bite of steak into his mouth. He chewed it as if it were a meditative exercise, slowly calming himself.

Then he continued: "You do not kill honest men who want only honest work for honest pay. You do not make women and children miserable for your profit. You do not swindle your countrymen!"

Here he took a large swallow of wine.

"I told them not to do this, and yet this is what they did. It was necessary to demonstrate my objection in the clearest way possible."

He took another long drink.

"I think that I have made my point to the ones that remain. They will not so easily ignore my advice from now on." He nodded, as if approving of what he'd just said—of how he'd handled the problem—and picked up his knife and fork for another bite of bloody beef.

I took a moment, trying to think of an appropriate response. Pablo possessed a fortress—a virtually impenetrable underground bunker on the south side of the Gulf of Mexico, in the small pueblo Chuburna, far away from the hectic pace of his headquarters in Mérida. He'd built it beneath an ancient stone temple, at the end of a scarred and rutted road, deep in the rain forest. It was there Pablo maintained an armory that put the munitions available to the entire Mexican military to shame, knowing that the government would never destroy the temple, it being such an integral piece of the nation's heritage. It was there that a security and surveillance operation to rival NASA's was centered. It was there, a hundred feet below the earth, encased in lead and powered by his own, personal solar field, that Pablo kept a subterranean mansion furnished in French antiques and a library of first editions, all set amid rose marble floors and pillars. This bunker was where the drug lords gathered, in the lap of luxury and Pablo's exquisite taste, when there was business to discuss—it was, in fact, where I'd been taken the year before to meet the heads of the cartels so I could pitch my money-laundering scheme to them. I wondered that Pablo hadn't called the lords together in this place to hash out their entry into the field of human trafficking. Lay down a few ground rules to make the operation humane. Set some standard fee for the service— a more affordable fee, if Pablo was so inclined.

When I'd met the group of them, Pablo's colleagues had seemed like such refined men—nothing as I'd imagined a bunch of Mexican drug lords would be—and there had seemed to be such amity

among them. Surely, they could have worked together to decide on terms that would have been
agreeable to all of them. Business was business,
and these were businessmen, interested above all
in profitability; they sold drugs for a living, after
all.

Before I could put all these thoughts in order
and work out a way to express them to Pablo without further agitating him, a shot rang out. I heard
it a nanosecond before the window we were sitting
in front of shattered, sending shards of tempered
glass flying onto our plates and into our hair.

There was no time to be stunned as this first
shot was followed by a barrage of more shots,
gunfire like fireworks. Still, I had enough presence of mind to dive to the floor, under the table
where Pablo had already taken cover. I skidded
on my way down, my Ferragamos leaving a streak
of blood on the terrazzo floor. It flashed through
my mind that the blood was from the steaks and,
just as instantaneously, I realized that only a naïf
could entertain denial like that. I started patting
myself, looking for a wound, thinking that, even
though there was blood, I couldn't be wounded
because I felt no pain, though that could be shock
—

"It's me," Pablo grunted.

I turned to where he was sprawled beneath the
tablecloth. He was bleeding from his shoulder, a
stain of red spreading on the pristine white of his
linen suit. "Oh, Jesus," I breathed. On instinct,
because the bullets were still flying above us and
there was no room in my adrenaline-fired brain for

rational thought, I reached from under the table to grab the napkin that had fallen from my lap when I'd dived, ripped Pablo's jacket open and pressed it hard into the gaping hole just under his collar bone.

There was so much blood. The only other time I'd seen a quantity of blood like this was the evening I'd walked into my guest room in Pablo's bunker and found one of the drug lords—the beautiful maniac, Alvaro—beheaded in my bed. I rethought my observation about the fellowship among the thieves who were my colleagues; had Alvaro been the outlier I'd assumed, too danger-ous to be allowed to live even among criminals? Deserving of his demise? His death a relief, even if I'd have preferred it hadn't been accomplished on *my* feather bed? But who among the lords would mark *Pablo* for assassination?

The napkin was sopping with Pablo's blood al-most as soon as I pressed it to his wound, my shaking hands drenched in red. Pablo must have noticed my own blood had drained from my face. My quivering lips and hands. "Flesh wound," he assured me, grunting through gritted teeth. "Hurts like a son of a bitch though—"